PRAISE FOR LAURA

MW00929968

"I've read Laura's _____ ... and can attest to its power. It evokes the 1970s in a painfully accurate way, and is beautifully written. She manages a wide cast of characters and somehow paints adults, teenagers and children with equal skill without ever condescending to any of them. Her skill at characterization and turns of phrase, coupled with a great sense of place, makes this a heck of a novel."
-Tom Franklin

KNOW SMALL PARTS:
AN ACTOR'S GUIDE TO TURNING MINUTES INTO MOMENTS AND MOMENTS INTO A CAREER

"Laura has built a built a career by herself out of hard work and the ability to understand that in order for her to succeed she would have to adapt to the moments and times of her life. What makes her even more remarkable is that she never gave up her personal integrity in this most difficult business. She has absolute love, command and respect for the craft. She wants that thing that all actor's want. A part. A chance. It is with great respect that I salute her journey knowing that her life has been much more than just the movies. She has stopped her life and dreams multiple times to invest in others difficulties. Laura's outward beauty could have guaranteed her much more in this business perhaps even worldwide fame. She could have taken an easier route for her professional pursuits but instead chose to make it about the work and only the work. She is a role model in that regard and a true leading lady. Enjoy what she has to say and see if you can see yourself in her journey. She still has some big important parts to play."
-Kevin Costner

"She's nailed the daily life of an actor in L.A. about as perfectly detailed as it gets... You can say that Laura is amazingly correct in everything she says and sees, but she makes you hunt for the urgent need to do it which is at the bottom of all."
-Richard Dreyfuss

"Laura Cayouette is a working actress that also has a happy, well-balanced life. Figuring out how she manages this feat is certainly worth a read."

-Reginald Hudlin

"Anyone who has met Laura knows that she is unforgettable. Perhaps even more impressive is that she has found a way to translate this personal charisma and life-force into her appearances on screen, making the most of every second of camera time given to her. She has literally figured out a way to bottle lightning. I'm sure that her observations and guidance will be invaluable to the actor who is looking to make his or her mark in the film world and to build a career, moment by moment."

-Lou Diamond Phillips

"Laura Cayouette's *Know Small Parts* is required reading for everyone with stars in their eyes. Hollywood is inundated daily with countless dreamers hoping for a career in front of the camera, but no idea how best to pursue one. Laura's smart, sensible and no nonsense step by step approach to achieving a career as an actor is certain to be the new bible for everyone yearning to break into the biz. I look forward to Laura being thanked in many future Oscar speeches."

-Adam Rifkin

ALSO BY LAURA CAYOUETTE

FICTION

Lemonade Farm

NON-FICTION

Know Small Parts: An Actor's Guide to Turning Minutes into Moments and Moments into a Career

How To Be A Widow: A Journey From Grief to Growth
(editor only)

LAtoNOLA
blog - latonola.com

PREFACE

In an effort to capture the unique culture of New Orleans, many of the people and places mentioned in this fictional novel exist in reality. As such, you can trace Charlotte Reade's steps and enjoy many of her experiences for yourself. In an effort to entertain, I've sometimes bent these real people and places to my fictional will so "real life" experiences may differ.

I have included an Appendix listing many of the restaurants, tours, people and events mentioned in this novel along with links to their sites. For more information and photos on anything mentioned in this book, use the search tool in LAtoNOLA (latonola.com), the blog upon which many of the book's recollections are based.

I've also built a playlist of music videos and videos of parades and other events, places and people included in this story on my YouTube channel:
https://www.youtube.com/user/latonolawordpress

You can link directly to the playlist at:
http://bit.ly/1YerEFQ

And I've created a clipboard of photos on Pinterest:
https://www.pinterest.com/latonola/the-secret-of-the-other-mother/

Enjoy!

For "The Three Wise Men."
Quentin who told me to write it,
Ted who read every page as I wrote it
and Andy who supported me all along the way.
Thank you.

In loving memory of
Rosa Lee Jackson
"Dee"
with gratitude
for generations of "other mothering."

LA to NOLA Press

© 2016 Laura Cayouette

ISBN-13: 978-1522992608
ISBN-10: 152299260X

First Edition: April 2016

Back cover photo by Robert Larriviere

Many of the people and places mentioned in this fictional novel exist in "real life." At times, the author has bent these real people and places to her fictional will. Although the author has made every effort to ensure the accuracy and completeness of much of the information contained in this book, we assume no responsibility for errors, inaccuracies, omissions, or any inconsistency herein. Any slights of people, places, or organizations are unintentional.

THE SECRET OF THE OTHER MOTHER
A Charlotte Reade Mystery

Laura Cayouette

Chapter 1

I didn't start acting young like most people but I was still wistful enough to think red carpets would be like in the movies - all popping flashbulbs and elegance. That was fifteen years ago. Now I knew red carpets were mostly about yelling.

"Charlotte, this way!" "Charlotte, show us the back of the dress!" "Charlotte! Charlotte!!!"

I had dreamed about this particular red carpet for nearly eight years. We were going to make the greatest sexual drama since *Last Tango in Paris*. Heck, we were going to singlehandedly bring back the genre. And this time I was more than one of the actors, I was one of the movie's producers. I turned to the left and smiled at shouting photographers, then to the right and smiled some more, but I knew our movie was no good. In fact, the critics hated it. Many called it "misogynistic" and said we were contenders for worst movie of the year.

So I wore the most daring dress I could find. Mom taught me early that if you have a pimple on your face, it's never a bad idea to wear a lower neckline. I'd taken that advice to an extreme wearing a scarcely-there dress festooned with feathers and chains. I was going to survive this pimple of a movie if it stripped me bare. Hell, I'd worn even less than the movie's female lead.

Sofia was waiting for me, her own camera in hand. "Charlotte! Charlotte! Show us some sideboob!"

I'd known Sofia since high school and it always anchored me to find her still-angelic face in all of this tinsel. I stopped at the end of the carpet and struck a pose for her. "I shouldn't have let you talk me into this dress. I can't even wear underwear. I'm commando on the carpet."

"You look amazing. What does your mom always say? 'Beauty knows no pain.'"

"Fine." I checked to make sure my breasts were still covered. "Ready to watch eight years of my life disappoint my industry?"

"Look at the bright side - it's poorly attended."

I laughed. "Right. So I only have to watch it baffle and offend dozens of anxious viewers."

"Right." Sofia smiled her light-up-a-room smile. "Come on."

The true measure of our movie's failure was that Clarence didn't have an after-party. He'd been there since the day we came up with the project - our shining white knight. If Clarence Pool wanted to make your movie, the world was your oyster. Only we turned our opportunity into crap. And there was the financial hammering I took after multiple backstabbings, betrayals and humiliations. Only Clarence had stayed true to his word the whole way through. I had my producer credit on our misogynistic movie. But no after-party. That was a bad sign.

The one bright spot was that a few of the critics actually loved me in the one scene that made the final cut. A few only loved me and hated everything else about the film. It wasn't much but it was something. I was going to read the reviews one more time before I went to bed.

The light on my machine was blinking and I pressed play. "You have three messages." Beep. "Hey Charlotte, it's Sonja. I can't make it to Support Ho's tomorrow. Tell the girls I said hi and eat a pancake for me." Beep.

"Hey, it's Marilyn. Sorry I couldn't make your premiere but I saw the dress. It's already on the web. You're crazy for wearing it but I think you may have started something." Beep.

"Charlotte? It's your cousin Lillibette. Sassy died... She was just old. The funeral is this weekend. Mama can't take you at her house 'cause there's already a bunch of people commin' in but I can get you a discount at the Royal Sonesta and you can move into Mama's after it empties out. Call me. I'm up."

I looked at the time. I was home unfashionably early at almost-midnight, 2 a.m. in New Orleans. I dialed then took a deep breath. "Lillibette?"

"Oh, hey cuz. You got my message? Yeah, she passed. Eighty-six. Mama's doin' okay but May's losin' it as you probably guessed. She's past the point. I passed out sedatives like they were breath mints. So, I was thinkin' you could stay at the Sonesta for a few days and then go to Mama's. We're in the middle of movin' or I'd love to have you here. Jonathan says hi."

"Hi Jonathan."

"Charlotte says hi. So, come, right? I'll pick you up at the airport. We can get you a copy of the death

3

certificate if you need it. I'm makin' my Dr. Pepper pineapple ham for the repass."

"Well then I guess it's settled."

Chapter 2

Lillibette was a talker. The stars of her stories were my family and their lifelong friends so listening to her was like flipping through photo albums where one detail could bring back a flood of memories. "I saw that actor come off your plane, the one who's in all those weird, funny movies. They're always so much shorter in person. You must tower over that city like the 'Fifty Foot Woman.' Sassy's twins're commin' in for the funeral. I can't even think the last time you would've seen 'em. When you were eight? Nine? It has to be a hundred years by now. Y'all won't even recognize each other. I guess they coulda seen you in some of your movies or somethin'."

"I figured out once that there was a four or five year period where I was on TV somehow everyday. Commercials, reruns, whatever. So, people don't really know who I am but they always think they met me at a party or something. I'm familiar."

"Well, they're commin' in and Mama said…" Lillibette kept on about Sassy's twins then talked about a time she saw me in a magazine and told the cashier she was my cousin. Outside my window, the city was rebounding. The Superdome gleamed in the distance. A billboard read, "Bless Our Boys" next to a black-and-gold fleur de lis logo.

Lillibette pointed to the billboard. "They're

thirteen and O now. Have you been watchin'?"

"The Saints?"

"Who Dat, baby! We're goin' all the way this time. Mama's goin' out of her mind. She can't believe Daddy's missin' all this. She keeps callin' him into the room when they're about to make a touchdown - just for good luck. He hadn't shown yet though. But honestly, even dead he's gotta know they're winnin'. Undefeated! We are going to do some serious dancin' in the streets when they win the Super Bowl."

"We don't really watch football in L.A."

She laughed loud and took a sip from her drive-thru daiquiri. "You heard they made this illegal? Now, we're supposed to leave the paper straw cap on or we get an open-container ticket. Can you believe that? The Feds think we're children, can't figure out for ourselves whether we can handle a cold beer on a hot day. Hell, I got higher off a swig of Maw Maw's cough syrup than I do off this Big Gulp of sugar water. But you don't really drink, do you?"

"Side effect of accidentally marrying an alcoholic."

"That was decades ago."

"I know, right?"

We passed the hotel with the clarinet down the side and turned onto Canal Street. Palm trees reached up between passing streetcars painted red with yellow trim. Bus stops were crowded with people who worked too far away to walk home.

Bourbon Street was as it had been before The Storm. Neon signs competed for attention with strippers in doorways flirting with bead-wearing, plastic "Hand Grenade" drink-cup-toting tourists.

One pretty girl in a bikini had "13-0" written on her cheek.

Music was everywhere. Live bands playing covers of 80's music, boom boxes blaring for street performers, brass bands playing local-grown standards, D.J.'s spinning crowd favorites, hipsters with ironic hair choices playing random instruments and children tapping with Coke cans smashed under their sneakers. I loved it.

We dumped my bag in the room then headed out for a bite. In Los Angeles, you learn to ignore things like a mass of paparazzi swarming the H&M next to you because Lindsey Lohan is shopping. In New Orleans, you learn to keep a conversation while passing groups of young women dressed in matching veils and tutu's or a man waving a giant sign reading, "BIG ASS BEERS." We joined the line at The Gumbo Shop and took off our knit caps. Gumbo is one of those dishes everyone's mama makes. So even if you don't like a particular version, you have to respect gumbo because every gumbo tastes like somebody's mother's gumbo.

Lillibette waved at a wedding parade passing in the street. "We're doing the second line day-after-tomorrow. Mama went all out. She even got an Indian. Well, TinaBee did - you know, Mama's housekeeper's girl. She arranged it all really. LilBee helped and got the brass band from BigBee's funeral. I don't think you ever met BigBee but it was a nice second line. Good parade. Fun. She'd of liked it. It's not too long a route but wear comfortable shoes to the funeral."

I caught a tourist listening to our conversation.

They looked really confused.

And that's the face I pictured on Sofia as I tried to explain the local funeral traditions to her on the phone after my "3-cup sampler" gumbo dinner. (Two were pretty good). "The 'first line' is the family and the band, the people involved in the wedding or the funeral or whatever. The 'second line' is all the people who join the parade along the way."

She giggled. "So people just invite themselves to your family funeral or your wedding?"

"They join in. I don't know how else to explain it. They wave kerchiefs or cocktail napkins and join the party."

She was full-on laughing now. "Of the funeral."

"Yes, the funeral parade. Okay, I heard it that time. That sounds weird. But, yes. The parade to mourn your loss. Then the music gets faster and funkier and they celebrate the life of the person and their return home. You'd love it. They put the fun in funeral here."

"Don't tell my sister. She's going to insist we throw her some huge one with, like, Pantera as the band." Sofia was cry-laughing now.

"With an Indian."

"Yes, with an Indian! Wait, why is there an Indian?" She could barely get the words out from cry-laughing. But she did this all the time. It was one of my favorite things about her.

How could I possibly describe an Indian and make it make sense that you'd have one in your funeral parade? "A Mardi Gras Indian. I'd have to remember the whole story of them but there are just no words to describe their beauty. They wear these huge, elaborate beaded and feathered suits that weigh up to a hundred pounds and take, like, a year to make. And they cost thousands of dollars and most of the Indians don't have that kind of cash but it's so worth it when you see them. They look like a tribe as seen through, like, a super-colorful kaleidoscope with all these cultural concepts and histories beaded onto these massive walls of feathers. They're walking works of art. I can't describe it. This place has inspired so many writers but words are pitiful in the face of it. Anyway, my Aunt Ava got a Mardi Gras Indian. No, her housekeeper's daughter did. Anyway, it's cool. I wish you could be there."

"So that's tomorrow?"

"Day after. Tomorrow is hanging out with family across the lake. There will be eating. And lots of storytelling. It'll be good." She couldn't see it, but I smiled.

Sofia took a deep breath. "You sound happy. I'm glad you went. I think you need this. L.A. is bunk. Oh wait, did you check the web? You should Google yourself. That dress is all over the place. Front views, sideboob views, naked back views, face shots with those crazy feathers and the fur collar, all of it. There's even some foot fetish site with just your feet."

"Okay. That's... I don't know what that is. I mean it's all in the ether, right? Google hits or whatever? Does it mean something if a lot of people are looking at you in a dress?"

She hammered the point. "In foreign countries. Like, lots of them. People are looking at your sideboob globally."

"Really? That's probably good. Right? Wow, maybe I'll come out of this worst-movie-of-the-year thing okay."

She started giggling again. "I'm sure all those backstabbers are scratching their heads wondering how you managed to avoid getting any of the mess on you. They're probably like, 'But we tried so hard to destroy her.'"

"Drats, foiled again."

She laughed then got more serious. "No, but probably they don't care. They got their money and they got their movie made and they don't really care what happens to you. You served your purpose."

"Ugh."

"Yeah. Have fun at the funeral. Is that what you say? What do you say?"

I laughed. "That's fine. I'll call you after."

"Night."

I looked in my bag for comfortable black shoes then called it a night.

Chapter 3

My Aunt Ava's house was a mansion-like fortress bought after The Storm. Ava said she couldn't do another hurricane in the city. She packed up over a hundred years of family history and moved it into a steel-girder-enforced house on high ground - a gated golf course on the Tchefuncte River. Her oldest, May, took on the the old manor home in the Garden District like she was competing in a home-makeover reality show. She cut the house into three rental units and Ava's youngest, Lillibette, took over the management of the property. I was proud of them both but I was pretty sure I hated the idea of the family home being butchered.

I knew my two favorite stories about Sassy wouldn't be told at the memorial so I was glad to hear them both at Aunt Ava's. Everyone bustled around the kitchen setting out casserole dishes brought by neighbors, church goers and Bridge players. Ava sat in the breakfast nook in a tall, cushy armchair like a flaming-haired queen on her throne and recounted when she and Maw Maw had pulled up to that bus stop and Ava had seen Sassy standing there. Ava and Sassy were both teenagers at the time and exchanged a look through the open window. Maw Maw pulled over and yelled out the window, "Hey, girl!"

Sassy lowered her chin and looked left, then right, then back to the car. She walked slowly to the car and the next thing you know, she was raising three generations of this family, including my infant mother. That story never made a whole lot of sense to me, vacant as it was of any detail of the transaction that led to the blending of our family's lives. But I knew Sassy to be Mom's "other mother." Her round, sweet face and black-brown eyes were imprinted on all our hearts.

My mom told the one about how Sassy got her twins. Sassy had already found out that her husband wasn't really her husband on account of him being a bigamist. She'd had the vision about having children and told Mama Heck's ghost she was worried how she couldn't see their daddy's face. Then she went to the laundromat like she did every Saturday. She was just finishing her folding when a lady came in carrying a laundry basket with twin babies sitting on top. They were tiny with rich, fine skin and a light dusting of tight curls. Sassy told the lady they were adorable and the lady looked up, exhausted, and said, "You want 'em?"

And that's how Sassy got Taffy and Chiffon. I had no idea which one was hugging me when I walked into the church on Rampart. Half of the rows were filled with parishioners and friends. The twins settled in with their uncle, Paris, in the otherwise empty front rows. One twin wore her hair in long waves. The other had hers pinned up and piled high. On our side of the room were two rows packed with fair-haired, blue-eyed people - Sassy's other family. Paris was the only one in the building actually related to

Sassy.

The service was somber. The preacher spoke of "Sister Cassandra" like she was a warrior and a saint. Sassy was at least a little of both. People tended to cry hard and laugh hard around here. Several women fainted into the waiting arms of their sisters-in-faith. The preaching was peppered with shouts of, "Yes, Lawd!" and "Praise Him!" while women in stylish hats fanned themselves and raised hands to the ceiling. It was nice to openly cry. After a few years in New York and nearly two decades in Los Angeles, I'd gotten tougher. I always said, "If you want to play with the big boys, you gotta be able to take the big hits." I ran with some pretty big boys. Here, being soft came easier.

Sassy looked that way dead bodies do - herself and not herself. And bloodless. I looked at her face for the last time and tried to find her warm smile. It was gone. She was gone.

We lined up outside the church, the family up front, the brass band in the back. The musicians wore t-shirts that read "Hot 8." The trumpeter, a big strong guy with amputated legs, played and rolled his wheelchair down some of the most pot-holed and cracked streets in the country. Our parade moved slowly at first as we sang dirges like *I'll Fly Away*. Then the tempo picked up and the same lyrics suddenly sounded different to me. Sassy had a good life and her sorrows were over. Some things just have to be enough.

Sassy only had one request about her passing. She'd always said when it was all said and done, to dance down Elysian Fields because that's where she'd be. The Mardi Gras Indian danced in his beautiful suit of royal blue plumes reaching at least seven feet into the sky. People came out on their stoops and danced along to our band. The shop employees came out to see and waved when they spotted the photos of Sassy framed by peel-n-stick bows and held high on wooden sticks.

The music was infectious. People's feet moved in the shuffle steps of second line dancing. Sometimes, someone would drop and do splits. Maybe another dancer would stop and feign fanning them. Some men in matching suits carried elaborately decorated baskets and umbrellas. I was in the habit of walking with a parasol and was glad I'd thought to bring mine. I pumped it in the air to the beat like I saw the others doing.

I smiled at my mother, my brother, my aunt and my cousins. In L.A., I almost never got to see faces this familiar. Except Sofia, of course. I'd been smiling at her face since back when she was the new girl in high school.

We made our way to Sassy's shotgun house in the Treme and danced on the street outside for one last song. The tourists, strangers and neighbors we'd picked up along the route headed back toward the French Quarter as many friends hugged goodbyes and others followed me and the relatives through the house to the porch out back for the repass. Card tables held giant foil roasting pans of fried chicken, Lillibette's Dr. Pepper ham, potato salad, spiced green beans with onions, jambalaya, browned rolls and bread pudding. I fixed a plate then followed my mother inside.

We sat on the orange brocade couch and set our paper plates on the wooden coffee table in front of us. Pictures of President Kennedy and Martin Luther King, Jr. watched over us as we blessed the meal and dug in. I looked up to find Sassy's prized possession, her chandelier. It was only as wide as a large pizza pan but it was as regal as anything you'd find in a palace or house of state.

The wavy-haired twin sat with us and looked up as well. "That damn chandelier."

I was surprised to hear her assessment. "You don't like it?"

"It's beautiful… and Mama loved it." She smiled and shook her head like she'd just heard a private joke.

I finished chewing the crispy, tender batter-fried chicken. "It's a family treasure, right?"

She laughed. "More like a family ball and chain. We've been draggin' that thing around for four generations, since slave days ended."

My mom perked up, then wiped her mouth with her paper napkin before speaking. "Your family has had that chandelier since slavery? That must be a story."

The twin smiled and her nose wrinkled. "The story goes Mama got the chandelier from Mama Heck when she passed. But before that, Mama Heck got it from her mother, Mama Eunoe, who'd come down from a plantation in northern Louisiana. Mama Heck said her mama came by it honest. The lady what owned her gave it to her when she got freedom. She said keep it in the family. So we did."

My mother was clapping with excitement. "Your

great-grandmother carried that chandelier through the entire state of Louisiana to bring it here?"

"I think she lived in Texas when the war ended. But, yes. Hung it right there when she made her home in the Treme and lived out her days smiling up at it, if you ask Mama Heck." She pushed a pickle out of her potato salad. "Don't know how much longer we gonna keep it hangin' there. Might have to pack this place up."

"Oh my." My mother stopped eating. "Of course. You two don't even live in the city anymore, do you?"

"No ma'am. Chiffon lives in Baton Rouge and I stayed in Alabama after college. I'm teachin' there now."

So this twin had to be Taffy. I tried to memorize - Taffy equals wavy hair, Chiffon equals high hair.

"You should hear how I talk there - all college-professor-like. But it's Alabama so they let a lot slide accent-wise, ya' heard me?" Taffy shooed a fly from her plate. "When The Storm was comin' Mama wanted to take it with her, the chandelier. UncaParis told her she was crazy but she threatened all kinda things so he took the damn thing down and packed it in the truck rolled up in a blanket. Later, when she got back, she saw some woman on Oprah who'd taken her tiara with her. She said, 'See! I'm not the only one crazy enough to drag around finery.' It was this lady won 'Queen for a Day' on Oprah years ago and Oprah gave her that tiara. She wore it all through hell and high water. I said, 'Mama, it's a tiny crown. You draggin' fifty pounds of breakable around.' Lawd, she was stubborn." Taffy's head lowered under the weight of her loss.

Mom slid her empty plate under mine. "Wasn't it a beautiful day for a parade? Breezy and warm on a December day."

Taffy gave Mom a tiny smile. "Yes ma'am."

Mom opened the dime store photo album on the coffee table and thumbed through it. "Oh, wasn't she darling?" She pointed to the cherubic tot sitting on Mama Heck's generous lap. There were only a couple more photos of Sassy growing up along with ticket stubs from a prom, a movie house and a torn stub with "The Dream" written in fancy script before the tear. I cried a little when I saw the photos from my cousin May's wedding. I had taken the pretty shots of Sassy fastening May's necklace and even spotted myself in the mirror in one photo. It made me feel special knowing Sassy had something of mine on her coffee table. I always found new reasons to be glad I was such a shutterbug.

I tried explaining the second line parade to Sofia that night. She kept "trying to get a mental picture," but mostly failed. New Orleans is mostly a you-had-to-be-there city. I couldn't even make jambalaya make sense over the phone. The closest I got was, "It's like paella, only totally not."

Sofia especially loved the names - Mama Eunoe, Mama Heck, Taffy, Chiffon, Paris and Sassy. "Those are their real names? Like, on their birth certificate?"

"I know Sassy was from my mother being too little to say Cassandra, but I think the rest are really their names. Mama Heck is probably short for something, but who knows? Her mom might have just gotten tired of naming children and said, 'Aw heck,' and that was it."

Sofia started giggling. "Did she have more kids? Is there a Papa Damn-It out there somewhere?"

"Mama Not-Again!"

Sofia was really laughing now. I could barely understand her through the spasms. "Papa Just-Stop-Already!"

We laughed until we calmed down. I could hear Sofia's three-year-old, Nia, talking to her toys in the background. I broke the mood. "Tomorrow's the reading of the will. I was a little surprised Sassy had thought ahead like that. I guess a lot of people did after the The Storm. Anyway, Mom and Ava have to be there so I'm going. I've never been to one before. Have you?"

"A will reading? No. Maybe it'll be fun. Maybe you'll learn something cool about her."

"Maybe."

I checked my email before turning in. The one from my manager, Marilyn, was entitled, "OPEN THIS!" I couldn't tell if she'd forgotten to turn off the "Caps" or if THIS WAS REALLY IMPORTANT!

"THAT DRESS WAS THE BEST DECISION YOU EVER MADE! IT'S EVERYWHERE! YOU'RE EVERYWHERE! YOU'RE TRENDING! COME BACK SOON!"

I still couldn't tell if it was REALLY IMPORTANT! I clicked "mark as unread" and went to sleep.

Chapter 4

I wasn't sure how to dress for a will reading. Judging from the Saints jersey the attorney was wearing under his suit jacket, I guessed my $300 jeans were just fine. Mom looked at them the way Maw Maw would have - like they were "dungarees" worn by field hands. Lillibette thought they were cute.

I understood most of what was going on but only because I watched an insane amount of *Law & Order* and spoke a little "legalese." The house would go to the twins. The insurance, modest accounts and family Bible would go to her brother Paris.

I knew Aunt Ava not-so-secretly wanted the chandelier for her dining room but she seemed more than happy to receive-back Maw Maw's ruby and pearl collar necklace with the clasp so ornate it could be worn at the front. Mom is always happy to receive any gift of any kind so she clapped her hands and squealed when she inherited Sassy's quilt made with Mama Heck's wide, strong hands. I knew the first thing Mom would do is smell the quilt to see if she could find Sassy there. Then she'd probably clap her hands some more. A few more friends and neighbors received sentimental gifts - a Lenox statue of Mary, a dozen colorful church hats, the Henkel knife set my uncle gave Sassy one Christmas and a crystal punch bowl were among her treasures.

Then the Saints-fan attorney read the special provisions and requests. "I'm leaving the care of our family chandelier to my daughters, Taffy and Chiffon. You must keep the chandelier in the family. Y'all know I'd rather keep it in Louisiana but it MUST hang in our family home for all generations to come. You know I'm watching.

I did my best with y'all. I think we got mostly lucky. I hope y'all would say the same. I'm sorry for anything you didn't get. I did all I could to give y'all a name that meant something. I understand if that isn't enough. Follow your hearts and you will never betray me. Except with the chandelier. Take your best care of the chandelier."

I whispered to Mom. "She's pretty serious about that chandelier."

Mom exhaled a laugh through her nose. "I'd say so."

Afterward, we sipped from Dixie cups of cucumber water as papers were signed. Taffy and Chiffon were in a corner having an energetic conversation. Mom and Ava came up to me holding hands. Their age gap sometimes made them look like a grown teen-mother and daughter but right now they looked like school girls. Mom nudged Ava and Ava looked right at me. "We think you should stay for Christmas. Your mother has already agreed to stay so it would nearly be sacrilege to leave."

"Like spitting in my face." Mom grinned mischievously. "Just say yes."

We exited then pooled again in the parking lot. Taffy told no one in particular, "There's still plenty of food at the house if y'all wanna come by." Mom and Ava decided to go on ahead and Lillibette invited herself to crash at my hotel after going to at Sassy's to eat leftovers from the repass.

The chandelier sparkled in the late-day sunlight streaming through the nearly-floor-to-ceiling window next to Sassy's front door. It really was beautiful. The spine dripped with hundreds of nickel-sized round crystals. Mirrored fleur de lis crystals dangled amid the luminescent teardrops hanging below the dozen electric candles. More teardrops and rounds hung from the top, where the lamp is meant to meet the intricately and ornately carved ceiling-medallions standard in most old manor homes.

Taffy offered me a seat and took the lounge chair her mother usually chose. "Did you want some food?"

"I think Lillibette's helping Chiffon set it all out. We'll go in a minute. How are you doing? Was that weird for you?"

Taffy leaned back in the lounger. "That's the perfect word for it. You were always good with words. Yeah, it was weird."

"Good weird or bad weird?"

Taffy laughed and pushed her wavy hair behind her ear. "Good, I guess." She paused a minute. "Chiffon and I are thinking of findin' our other mother, the one what birthed us."

"Really? What brought that on? Is this, like, a new thing?"

"We've thought about it through the years but Mama said it was best if we could find a way to let it go."

"Wow. That's kinda ominous." I was never sure how much truth to tell when something seemed clear to me, but I always tried to be diplomatic. "It sounds like she was trying to protect you."

"Probably. Yeah, she was like that. But, it sounded like Mama was givin' us permission to look now she's passed."

"Really? How so?" I had just been trying to be a good friend but now I was genuinely intrigued.

"All that stuff about tryin' to give us a name and understandin' if that wadn't enough. She said, 'Follow your hearts and you will never betray me.' She was sayin' we could look if we wanted. Chiffon thinks so too."

I wished I understood more but stayed agreeable. "Sounds like it. You'd know better than I would. Did she ever mention betrayal before?"

Taffy looked toward Chiffon busying herself in the kitchen, then back at me. "It just felt wrong, ya' heard me? She never said 'betrayal,' we did. We accused her of holdin' back, you know? Like she was keepin' stuff from us because she was afraid we'd like the other mother more."

I sat forward on the couch. "Wow, what did she say?"

"She shook her head like we was pitiful."

"Oh." I closed my eyes and shook my head a few times, trying to find the right head-shake for pitiful. I looked at Taffy then shook my head like she was pitiful. It felt like I nailed it.

Taffy jolted. "Oh, that's crazy. How you gonna look just like her like that?" She yelled to the kitchen. "Chiffon, come out here and see this!"

22

Chiffon came out of the kitchen with Lillibette just behind her in the doorway. "What?"

Taffy smiled at me, "Go on, show her. Chiffon, tell me if this ain't Mama after we told her we thought she was afraid we'd betray her. Go on, Charlotte, do it."

I looked at Chiffon and, in my head, I heard her telling me that I was afraid she would like that other woman more than me. Then I shook my head at her like she was pitiful.

"Oh shit!" Chiffon covered her mouth then said to the walls, "Oh, I'm sorry. I didn't mean to curse in this house, Mama, but damn! How did you do that?"

"I'm a way-overtrained actor. I found the right head shake then worked backward. I just tried to think what would make your mama do that? What was she thinking? Where did the pity come from? Stuff like that."

Taffy was looking at me like I'd just pulled a rabbit out of my hat. "You ask a lotta good questions, you know that? Chiffon, she just pulled all this betrayal talk out of me in less than three minutes. You ever told anyone that shit?" Chiffon shook her head no. "Me neither. I'm not in the habit of telling my bizness. Next thing I know, this pale skinny lady is giving me Mama's look-o-pity. You're like a sorceress or somethin' Charlotte. Does she do that to you, Lillibette?"

Lillibette was happy to be included. "She comes by it honestly. Her mama used to be a therapist and her daddy's a spy so she sees stuff about people. Plus she studied at some famous acting academy in New York and she still takes classes to this day. Right?

You still take those classes? There are all these famous people in her class. RuPaul, that kid from *Married With Children*, Tyra Banks, all kinds of people. Didn't you do a scene with Pauly Shore?"

"Yep."

Taffy and Chiffon didn't look too clear on who Pauly Shore might be. Taffy stood up and headed for the kitchen. "Let's fix a plate. Lillibette, they ate every last bite of that ham you made. Scooped the sauce out with a spoon and poured it over the potato salad and rubbed rolls in it. Charlotte, are you staying for Christmas?"

Lillibette spun at me. "Yes. Say yes."

"I'm thinkin' about it. Does seem silly to go back to that soul-sucking town for Christmas when I could be in the belly of my family surrounded by the people who love me most. Plus, my mom's staying. I don't get to see her enough now that she left Louisiana again."

Lillibette high-fived Taffy. "Settled. You're stayin'. Done and done. Tate's room at Mama's opens up tomorrow. You can stay there. Great, let's eat."

I didn't check my messages until we got back to the hotel. It was Marilyn. Again. "Lillibette, do you mind if I make a call?" She waved me off and headed out the door with the ice bucket. No telling what she planned to cool in there. I dialed. "Hey Marilyn."

"Oh my God, you're killing me! When are you coming back? The dress is blowing up. I'm getting calls about you."

"Calls for work?"

"Mostly wanting to touch base. A few people seemed open to a meeting. But, I'm telling you, everyone knows who you are right this minute and this minute is going to pass."

"The girl in the dress."

"What?"

"That's how they know me, as the girl in the dress."

"I know, I know, you studied Shakespeare, whatever. I'm telling you, right now, the girl you want to be in this town is the girl in that dress. Come home."

"I am home."

Marilyn laughed. "You know what I mean. Timing is everything. Right NOW is the time to be here."

I thought about what she was saying. I flashed forward through some general meetings with big wigs who weren't really working on anything at that moment, lunches with power-guys figuring out if they could get away with hitting on me and red carpets for movies I wasn't in with the expectation that I'd wear something even more outrageous. "I hear you. I do. Seriously. But, Monday is the twentieth. People aren't going to want to set up anything this week. Look, it's possible that this moment will pass by the end of the winter break. You and I both know no one's doing anything until after the New Year."

"I really think we're going to miss the window." She sounded anxious.

"I think you could be right. I'm agreeing with you. But, there's really nothing we can do about it. This is God's timing. This is the way it played out. I think we just have to accept it and have a good vacation. If it's meant to be, people will still like looking at my sideboob in 2010."

Marilyn laughed. Yay. She was passionate but could be reasonable at the end of the day. She just HATED taking no for an answer. Always. That's why she was such a great manager. "Okay, fine. Merry Christmas."

Lillibette returned with the ice and went through her bags.

I shot her the "one minute" finger. "Happy Chanukah."

Marilyn made her last move. "I'm calling you before the New Year to hear when you're coming back."

"Gotcha."

Lillibette was emptying individually-capped servings of Jello-shots into the ice bucket. "Wanna go out? It's Friday before game day. Good night to be on Bourbon."

And it was. The bar-lined street was crowded with people toting go-cups or sucking on giant booze-filled fish bowls hung on leashes around their necks. Lots carried those green plastic Hand Grenade drinks, designed to blow your mind I guess. Most wore black-and-gold. Some wore blue and white. Guys mostly sported Saints jerseys and hats. Women showed off home-grown cleavage in tight black-and-gold t-shirts. Many wore matching sparkly fascinators in their hair. I liked the tiny top hats with puffs of feathers and ribbons and tulle.

I felt like an idiot, or worse - a non-fan, dressed in my brown turtleneck and jacket with a turquoise scarf. I wasn't used to feeling embarrassed. I'd lived a fairly shameless life where I accepted that not everyone was going to like me or my choices. But I felt like a kid who'd forgotten to wear underwear to school. Black and gold? What was I going to wear to watch the game tomorrow? My mourning dress? I felt totally unprepared. I was so used to having the right costume for any occasion. I had packed so dang light thinking I was just going to be in New Orleans for a few days. If I was clever, I had enough tops and undies for almost two weeks of outfits. I'd probably have to hand wash some socks. Good enough.

A loose cluster of the blue-and-white-wearing people started yelling stuff at the black-and-gold people surrounding them for blocks. Then something amazing happened. A few black-and-gold people started chanting "Who Dat!?! Who Dat!?! Who Dat sayin' they gonna beat them Saints!" Suddenly, hundreds of people were chanting it, then it spread down Bourbon Street at least a block in either direction. Something in my body ached and I happy-cried a little at the beauty of it all, the unity. I'd been on movie sets when they tried to get hundreds of people to do the same thing at the same time. It takes a minor miracle to pull it off even after several rehearsals. This was just springing up from the pavement fully formed. It blew my mind.

I even got caught up and let myself chant it once I got the rhythm. I felt like a phony, a brown and turquoise-wearing phony, but it was too good a moment to let pass without catching a ride. Lillibette seemed to like it that I joined in and that was genuine enough for me.

Chapter 5

Mom was thrilled to hear I was staying for Christmas. Lillibette had plenty of good arguments for staying through New Year's and I was feeling pretty inclined to give in even though Mom was leaving before then. This trip to the thrift shop was meant to help convince me I could get plenty of clothes to stay. As least that's what Lillibette said on the streetcar ride uptown on stately live-oak-and-manor-home-lined St. Charles Ave.

The street the shop sat on was under construction. Normally, when a street is fixed in New Orleans, it looks just as old-fashioned afterward but on this street, they'd built modern concrete curbs and sidewalks. Normal-everywhere sidewalks complete with wheelchair ramps on the corners. But the shop was pure New Orleans. Rhinestone-bedazzled gowns in Christmas-inspired red and white crowded the windows accessorized with white furs, long satin gloves, peau de soie pumps, sparkly tiaras and extravagant costume jewelry. For the men, there were tuxedos, overcoats, top hats, formal gloves, fleur-de-lis-shaped cufflinks and shiny black shoes. I felt like I'd been invited to a ball. A sign above the door read, "On the Other Hand" and a bell jangled as we entered.

Teeming racks of gowns and fanciness filled the

floor. The owner was sitting behind a desk covered in fine things. A silver and crystal framed mirror sat with a silver filigree lipstick holder next to it. Semi-precious and costume rings towered and spilled over a crystal ring dish with a hand-written sign reading, "$10, 2 for $15" propped next to it. A table lamp decorated with dangling beads illuminated an old-fashioned phone, the kind with a spindly gold cradle for the gold-trimmed handset. A pen sat in a marble pen holder and was decorated with a foot-and-a-half-long ostrich plume dyed purple. An electric calculator, the old kind with buttons, seemed to be the only cash register. A metal ashtray was brimming with half-smoked slender cigarette butts. A long, well-manicured nail tipped ashes onto the pile then lifted to the elegant ruby-red mouth of Miss Kay Danné.

Miss Kay was wearing a satiny red and black print cocktail dress, a long strand of pearls, chunky costume-jeweled earrings topped with a scarlet hat festooned with abundant black feathers. Her dining room chair was stacked with mis-matched cushions under her and behind her back. She looked up from beneath her hat. "There's a whole 'nother room in the back. Super-discounted. Ninety percent off everything. Get a cookie. Enjoy the music."

We walked through a short hallway crowded with hat racks and cashmere sweaters and into a giant white, warehouse-like room with jam-packed racks pushed so close together that it was hard for me to pass even with my slender frame. An older man dressed as Santa offered us sugar cookies from a Christmas plate. "We have lemonade if you'd care for it." We took a couple of cookies and Santa placed the remaining goodies on top of a piano. He pulled his red pants up and sat to sing and play *Have Yourself a Merry Little Christmas* as we looked through racks of dollar wedding gowns and pretty dresses, sporty jackets and festive sweaters. It was easy to see how you could lose a day in this place. The prices were insane - $3 for a knit dress, $5 for a tweed jacket, $7 for a beaded purse, $1 for a crocheted hat. Yes, it would be okay if I ran out of clothes here.

Miss Kay was lighting another cigarette as we made our way out. "Did my husband get you a cookie?"

Lillibette waved. "Yes ma'am. It was delicious. Thank you."

"Come back soon. We'll be having another sale for the New Year." She put down her cigarette to wave.

The door jingled when I pulled it. "We will."

By the time we got back to the French Quarter, it was packed with football fans. I'd worn my only black-and-gold item, a poly-silk brocade dressy blouse with covered buttons atop skinny jeans and black high-heeled boots. Dodging spilled-beer-filled cracks and platter-sized potholes, I remembered why I never wore heels on Bourbon, especially this stupid, spindly kind. But I looked good and as Mom always said, "Beauty knows no pain."

We ducked into a bar called Fat Catz where happy people were moving their "apple-bottomed jeans" and drinking to excess. A tinny beat started and everyone in the bar shouted and pushed their way toward the dance floor. The song commanded them to get down and do their dance and suddenly the entire floor was moving in unison. When the chorus hit, Lillibette grabbed my hand and smiled as we moved our feet to the right, to the right then to the left, to the left. We kicked and kicked, moving along with the bar crowd. One thing I always loved about south Louisiana was that all the men dance, even alone or in groups without women. I found that sexy.

Then a whistle sounded and the place went bananas. An ominous band of horns was overtaken by hip hop then EVERYONE yelled along to *Stand Up & Get Crunk!* I had clearly found the team's anthem. The song's rappers used their deepest, scariest voices, "Here we come to get you. Here we come to get you." It was thrilling. I wanted to know all these rituals, to be one of the people screaming when I heard that whistle, face painted with "13-0" on one cheek and "Who Dat" on the other, wearing a tiny top hat and a fitted Saints t-shirt.

Lillibette tugged my arm. "We should leave if we want to get to Sassy's before the game." A fit guy wearing a black-and-gold sash that read "Dancing Man 504" jumped four feet off the ground right in front of us as we were exiting. There was always something new and marvelous to see here, to experience here.

As soon as we headed out of the Quarter, the streets were completely barren. Like, zombie-apocalypse barren. At first it was exhilarating walking down the middle of normally busy thoroughfares with not a car in sight. Then it got a little creepy as we realized even the cops would be watching the game if something happened to us. We started hearing bursts of cheering coming through the walls of people's houses.

"Shit! We missed kick off. Mama's gonna kill me if they lose. She's got a lot of rules about keepin' 'em winnin'. She doesn't want any of us jinxin' 'em. Bad juju."

"But it's fine if they lose, right? I mean, they're undefeated, right?"

"You know about this team, don'tya? Used to call 'em the Aints and some people would wear paper bags over their heads at the games outa shame for how terrible they were."

No one answered the door so Lillibette let herself in just as everyone was yelling at the TV. "Come on, y'all! What was that?" Taffy was up out of her seat bellowing.

Chiffon motioned for us to come in. "14-0 Dallas. I'm serious. They losin'."

Lillibette took in the TV screen. "Still first quarter. No worries, y'all."

Taffy gave us both hugs while she was up. "They just makin' it excitin'. Come in, fix a plate."

Lillibette hung her coat on a rack and reached out for mine. "I was just gettin' ready to tell Charlotte about Steve Gleason."

Chiffon's head dropped dramatically. "I love that man." She raised her hand to the ceiling, "Bless him," then looked up past her hand.

We peeled paper plates off a stack and filled them with various casseroles and pasta salads. Lillibette passed me a serving spoon. "So we'd been the Aints for like forever. Then Katrina happened and the team moved to Texas and things were all up in the air about the Dome, some people wantin' to run a wreckin' ball through it, some wantin' it to stand like how we stand. Anyway, they fixed up the Dome and finally brought the team back to the Dome in 2006 for the Atlanta game, those dirty birds. They had this huge concert with U2 and a bunch of other people and everyone that went said they had a blast because they had every reason to believe that the party would be the best part of the game.

So the game starts and nearly right away, there's this miracle moment. This guy, Steve Gleason, blocks a punt and the ball got run in for a touchdown. They say it was the loudest moment in the history of the Dome. The Saints ended up winnin' the game and then had a really good season, went to the Championship for the first time ever. People were so happy. All the time happy. It was great."

"We needed it." Chiffon motioned with a fork that the game was back on. "Him and Coach Payton and my man Drew Brees, bless them boys. True Saints."

Taffy slapped her outstretched hand, "Who Dat, baby!"

When the Saints were still losing to Dallas at halftime, people took turns saying "I believe. I believe." They kept on believing even as Dallas scored a third touchdown in the third quarter. When a Dallas field goal kick miraculously hit the field post, belief was at a fever pitch. I'd loved football as a kid but mostly because I wanted to please my father and accidentally became a fan. A pretty big one. What started with me being a human VCR, memorizing a game to tell my dad what happened while he was busy entertaining guests, grew to painting my face at

Terps games and making home cooked spaghetti for a few of the Redskins once in awhile. Then I moved to Los Angeles, where there is absolutely no football, and slowly forgot I even cared.

Though he still rooted for LSU like anyone from Louisiana, my dad had ditched the Saints for the Redskins in the 60's. I'm guessing it was some time around his first post-game water cooler discussion at his new job straight out of college. He'd already lost his accent by the time I was born. Mom's accent was still as thick and slow as molasses. I think that's why I'd always switched back and forth and was never sure which accent was "mine."

With ten seconds left in the game, I actually found myself believing that the Saints were going to get the game-tying score. I jumped up out of my chair with everyone else (Taffy had been standing for at least five minutes already) and held my breath. Everyone squealed as the play began, then quickly turned to panic as some Dallas dude sacked the beautiful Brees and the ball popped loose.

"Get it!"

But we didn't. Dallas took a knee and served the Saints their first defeat of the most amazing season they'd ever had. Taffy looked inconsolable. "Damn."

Chiffon started gathering plates. "No matter. It just woulda been lagniappe if we went undefeated. But it don't matter. We still goin' all the way. I believe!"

Taffy joined her. "I believe!" She ran to the door and yelled out to the street. "I believe!" Chiffon and Lillibette joined her. "I believe!" I crowded in. "I believe!"

Then from down the street, we heard it, "Who Dat!"

We laughed. "Who Dat!"

It went on for a couple minutes with more neighbors and passers-by joining in. In Los Angeles, people would burn thrash cans and overturn cars when the Lakers would win and here, people were having fun and celebrating when their team lost.

Back at the hotel, Lillibette washed her face and I checked my emails. Junk, junk, wait - an audition notice from Marilyn. There was a movie shooting here and the director would be here for a location scout in three days and was willing to read me while he was in town. Yay! Maybe I wouldn't miss my moment after all.

Chapter 6

As always, I was prepared to do what I could to blow this director away. I wore my mourning dress to suggest the expensive cocktail dress described in the script. I would've worn something more figure-fitting if I'd had my clothes from home and hoped he was that rare kind of guy who thinks covering up is sexy. I felt a little weird about meeting him in his hotel room so I was a bit grateful to find two other guys to please in there.

The guy sitting behind a table nodded his head at the chair opposite him. "I'm Derek"

The two guys piped up. "Josh." "Vince."

I waved once around as I sat. "Hi. Charlotte. Great view. You know there's a great restaurant just around the corner from here, Palace Cafe, if you haven't already tried it."

Derek looked up from his script. "Okay, any questions?"

"No, I think I got it." I razzled and dazzled best as I could with the three pages I'd been given.

Derek looked to the other guys. "Good work. I think we got it. Thanks for coming in." I hated it when I couldn't tell if I'd done well in the room. Usually, I'd know if I killed it or if I'd made some sort of off-putting misstep. But I'd learned long ago that you can book a job when you bombed an audition and watch as some bigger name gets the part when you killed it. It was an anything-can-happen kind of business.

I left the hotel hugging my jacket closed and wishing Mom hadn't already left. It would've been nice to get a hug during one of these moments of doubt. Unless you're a child, it's not like how it is in those talent shows on TV where the families are waiting in the wings with signs emblazoned with your name in glitter. At least I didn't have to leave with the dread that my meter had expired and the parking vultures had gotten me with their $40 tickets. No car, no worries.

I took Royal Street back into the Quarter to meet Lillibette for lunch. She stood in front of the Rouses Market enjoying a jazz band with a clarinet soloist who reminded me of a lunch lady at my middle school. Tiny braids peeked out between the clarinetist's knit hat and scarf. She was great and clearly loved to play. Lillibette waved then pointed to the building behind her. "Hey! Ain't der no mo."

"What?"

"The Royal Cafe. Ain't der no mo. That's what you say. So much washed away. Years after The Storm, businesses still shutterin' over it."

I looked at the rustic brick building across the street with a wrought iron balcony. It had been one of my favorite haunts for years. "What is it now?"

"Gift shop, looks like."

I was suddenly sad. "Damn. I loved that balcony. The food was always whatever, but I could sit up there for hours watching the world go by and listening to one-man bands and stuff. Damn. I was going to solve all the problems of the world on that balcony. I was going to sit up there at least once a year until I died. Gifts? Like tourist stuff?"

"Nice stuff. Fleur de lis things and candles with local smells. Come see."

"No. Not yet. I don't want to like it. Right now I want to hate it."

"Yeah… Beignets?"

"Medicinal usage. Anti-depression drug." Sometimes it would be years between my trips to Cafe du Monde. I would be certain their French donuts were one of the best things that ever happened to my mouth. Then, I'd find a sticky table and order a plateful and be just as certain there was no way they could taste as good as I remembered. They're just fried bread with powdered sugar, I'd tell myself, how good could they be? Then I'd bite into one and remember that this happened every time. They really were just so good when they were still hot and the sugar stuck in clumps to the browned skin. Yum. I washed it down with hot chocolate as Lillibette sipped on a cafe au lait. I liked thinking about my mom and dad courting at these tables during college, Maw Maw and Paw Paw taking Mom here as a toddler. Maw Maw's mother doing the same when Maw Maw was a tot.

Lillibette's mouth was still full and a tiny cloud of powdered sugar puffed from her lips when she spoke. "Oh! How was the audition?"

"No idea. I mean, I liked what I did but I made some offbeat choices so I'm not sure if I'm what they're looking for. Whatever. It was fine, I guess."

Behind the railing, a petite woman in a cute,

flared coat rested a black violin under her chin. An elegant trail of pale flowers, maybe cherry blossoms, was carved into the violin's wood. The woman's cargo-pant wearing costar sat on a foldout chair and strummed a strange rectangular black guitar. As soon as the bow hit the strings, it was obvious the violinist was a woman with choices. She was at least as good as any soloist I'd ever heard in any concert hall. It was kind of staggering. The guitarist smacked her hand on her guitar like it was a bongo. She was remarkable, serving as rhythm, percussion and guitar soloist. They played *Hotel California* and it was exquisite. The beignet eaters couldn't resist singing along. Everyone got really loud for the part about bringing the wine.

There are some songs I know every word of but have never really heard. As we raised white-enameled coffee cups and sang, I heard the words I was saying. I imagined myself running, trying to find a passage. I heard the night man say, "Relax," knowing I was trapped.

The duet took off into a high-energy battle of strings. I looked at Lillibette. "That song's kinda creepy. Why can't they leave? What'll happen if they try? Will the building stop them or the employees? Or some sort of forcefield? Or maybe you can leave the place physically but you can never not really just be stuck there. For eternity. Maybe it's like Satre's *No Exit*."

"You ask so many questions. I couldn't even make myself wonder all that."

"It's a habit."

She laughed. "It'd wear me out."

The women played *Eleanor Rigby* as the crowd sang about lonely people. Only for the first time in a long time, I didn't really see many lonely people. A few of the waiters in paper hats and sugary aprons looked a little worse for wear but that was about it.

Walking back to the hotel through Jackson Square, we passed tarot readers and other late night purveyors sitting at candlelit card tables. Back in the room, Lillibette decided to take a hot bath and I dialed Sofia. I hoped the ringer didn't wake Nia.

"Hey! How's New Orleans?"

"You really have to come here one day. You can't begin to believe this place. We just came from eating the world's best beignets while these two girls, one on violin and the other on guitar, got everyone in this giant place that only sells one thing to all sing along. And they were insanely good. They should be playing the Kennedy Center and they're like, propped on the sidewalk outside a donut shop. And earlier, there was this woman just killin' it on the clarinet. She was a badass, but she looked like someone's mom or something. Like a lunch lady."

"Sounds like they've got cool women down there."

"I haven't seen a fake boob in a week. It's awesome. And people dress like children when they're children and like grown adults when they're in their sunset years. Except during Mardi Gras. Then all bets are off. And Easter and, like, most holidays. And now it's all about game day. Holy cow, Sofia, football is like, the biggest thing here right now. I mean, football is always in the top of southern priorities - it goes; family, food, football and always

God. But this is next level. This is like the whole city is in agreement about one thing. And this city has had more than its fair share of disagreements. On the streets, people don't even say hi anymore, they wave and exchange 'Who Dats.'"

"What are hoodats? Is that like money or something?"

"No, like who dat? Like who dat sayin' de gonna beat dem Saints?"

She was trying so hard to follow. "The Saints are the football team?"

"Yeah but it's like they really are saints. I mean, I'm sure they're just regular guys but what they're doing for this city. I can't explain it but you feel it everywhere. The whole city and everyone in it is black-and-gold. There are signs in everyone's windows that say, 'I Believe.' And they really do. They believe this team that has sucked forever is going to the Super Bowl. People know all the words to all the songs they play for the games. They all do the dances too. It feels like 385,000 people all moving to the same beat at the same time. It's amazing, like a drug or something. Like a great date."

"How are the guys there?"

"Off my radar. The last thing I need is to meet some guy 1,800 miles from L.A."

"You could use them for target practice, polish your dating skills."

"I could write a book on dating."

Her giggle kicked in. "Yes, only it would be too sad. No one would read it."

I laughed. "No, they'd read it then blow their brains out."

I'd gotten her laugh going. "You could sell it to those bad-date guys!"

"That's terrible. I liked some of those jerks. I'd give it to them as gifts."

She calmed herself. Or maybe it had gotten too dark to be funny anymore. She took a big breath and blew it out. "Seriously, if you meet a guy there, you should go out. It could be fun. You always say the secret to life is knowing what to say yes to, so if some southern guy asks you on a date…"

"Say yes."

"Yes. Wait, did you get the movie?"

I started getting undressed. "I doubt we'll hear from them before the New Year."

"Well, you never know."

"Nope. Never do."

Chapter 7

We didn't draw names in our family. Pretty much everyone got presents from everyone. Now that we had another generation of children, my cousins' grandchildren, the pile of presents took up a third of Aunt Ava's well-appointed sitting room. I helped with passing out the boxes and bags bedecked with curled ribbons and colorful bows. It took awhile.

I had made DVD's for everyone, personalized montages of photos and videos from throughout our lives as a family, all set to fun and meaningful soundtracks. It had taken me months to compile and edit them. We watched the one I'd made for my aunt and cousins and everyone loved it. They laughed, they cried and I felt like a million bucks.

After, the kids ran around hopped-up on sugar and wearing out new toys as we finished laying out the buffet on the kitchen island. Aunt Ava stirred a half stick of butter into each pot on the stove before serving them. There was fried turkey and baked ham, Spinach Madeline, Oysters Rockefeller, green bean almondine, sweet potato casserole with marshmallows on top and so much more. Growing up with food this good, it was inevitable that I would come to associate food with love. And between that and my world travels, it was inevitable that I would have a vast knowledge of and appreciation for food.

We filled $300 china plates and found seats at the super-long mahogany dining table decorated with a green silk runner cluttered with pine boughs, fragile Christmas balls, colored-glass votive candles, bowls of glimmering beaded fruits and a tall candelabra in the middle. I looked up to where I knew Aunt Ava wished she could hang Sassy's chandelier.

Ava led the blessing then we all dug in and splintered into different conversations, mostly about the Saints. Ava made an "Mmm, mmm" sound while sampling the pecan currant dressing. "Are you staying for New Year's?"

Mom popped out of her nearby conversation to insert, "She's staying."

I looked to Ava and laughed. "Mom's leaving in a couple days anyway. I might, though. I'm thinking about it. I'd rather be here to ring in the new year. Here people have actual fun, not just the kind of fun that looks good in photos."

Ava lifted her eyebrow and finished chewing. "I hear there's a lot of filming going on down here. Lillibette said you met with a director the other day. Seems like a girl could make a livin' right here where she oughta be."

"That's what I hear. But I'm not a big believer in what I hear. I know how to make money in L.A. Not many people can say that. I'm an actor in her forties. The work drop-off at my age is staggering. I'd really have to think about starting over in a new market."

"Just a bee for your bonnet." She took a sip from her fine crystal gold-banded wine goblet. "I'm so glad you were here for Sassy's service. The twins told me they've really enjoyed getting to know you more."

"They're great. Funny too. We had a great time watching the Dallas game. You know, they might look for their birth mother."

"Oh no. Really? No good can come of that."

I was sort of surprised she had such a fully formed opinion. "Why do you say that? Sassy said that thing in her will about them not being able to betray her. They're takin' that to mean she was giving them permission."

"Whoever that woman was, she gave her babies to a total stranger and watched them walk away into the ether. She never even asked Sassy's name. If she's even alive, she never wanted to be found and she never wanted to be able to find them. Trust me, the woman is cold-hearted trash."

"Maybe, but she's their cold-hearted trash. Do you know who she is? Is that why you're so against it?"

"I don't have to know to know what I know. They don't need to lose two mothers in one year. If they go lookin' for her, she'll either be dead or break their hearts. Believe that."

Someone at the table yelled out, "Who Dat!"

I hated to admit it, but she was probably right. Ava pushed an oyster shell aside to get at the food under it. "Sassy did what she could to give them a name that meant something. I wish that were enough."

"Yeah, what do you think she meant by that? I mean, Taffy means candy and Chiffon means either fabric or pie filling. I don't get it."

Ava smiled. "I think she meant their last name."

"Yeah, but that ended up being from bigamy so

it's not really their name. Does that sound fraught with meaning? Like, the kind worth mentioning from beyond the grave? I don't know. I think she meant something else. Something more. Maybe the woman's name was Candy Pie. Well, not that, but you know what I mean."

"Around here, it could be that." She laughed at her own joke. "Darlin', she didn't get the woman's name. How could she have given them names based on a name she didn't know?"

I thought for a minute. Nope, nothing. She had a point. Damn. "I thought I was onto something but you're probably right."

"No good can come of it."

"Yeah. But I don't know if the twins will rest without it. I wouldn't. If I were playing one of them, losing my mom might even make me obsessed."

She waved her hand until she swallowed. "Oh Lawd, not that. Those are two very determined girls. I wouldn't want 'em on my scent. Lawd, let 'em find a hobby."

She could always lighten my mood. Mom and I did the dishes after. We hadn't cooked. She handed me a serving platter to dry. "You seem so much happier here."

"That's why I plan to retire here. This is where I'm at peace. Especially New Orleans but maybe I'll be too old to feel safe moving to a new city. My plan is to live on the river."

She smiled. "Yes, with your friends and cousins who are either widowed or single."

"And we'll rock on the porch and crochet things while shirtless boys fan us."

"It's a perfect plan." We laughed and she passed another dish. "You're probably right. Most people grow more fearful with age and as you age your mind has a harder time retaining new information - while still being able to remember every word of a song from 1972. That makes it harder to adjust to a new way of life. And I can't believe they don't make you show a passport to enter south Louisiana. This place is another country. But you seem so much happier. Just something to think about. A bee for your---"

I jumped. "For my bonnet? So, Ava hits me with the whole Hollywood South thing and then you come in for the carpe diem closer? Mom, I just produced a movie with Clarence Pool! Critics hate it and it's opening in less than a hundred theaters but I got it made. That's... impossible. It took eight years of my life but it exists now where before there was nothing. Film is forever. And that handkerchief of a dress I wore has me on everyone's laptops. This is a moment. This is when you double down and finally make something of it all. I've been at this in since 1989 and I've been making a living at it for twenty years. Only one percent of actors make enough money to live. Yes, my car is ten years old and I don't own, I rent, and I shop at Marshall's and H&M but I'm in the same one percent as Tom Cruise. That blows my mind. I was thirty-one before I did my first movie. That's the age when most women are retiring - like it or not. But, I'm still here. Or there. In L.A. The other LA. You know what I mean."

She dried her hands and put her magical mother arms around me. It was the safest place in the world. "Darlin', you've been so brave and you've worked so hard. I think we just take it for granted that you'll be amazing at anything you do. If you wanted to stay here for awhile, we just assume you'd be amazing at it."

I lifted my head from her shoulder. "They took away my balcony. I was going to write the Great American Novel on that balcony."

"Who took it?"

"Katrina. Army Core of Engineers."

She rested my head back on her shoulder and we swayed. "You'll find a new balcony. There's always another balcony here, Suga'." She pulled away and went back to the dishes.

Lillibette padded into the kitchen in a robe and slippers. "Did Mama mention that we have a room opening in Casa Tate?"

I pointed to Mom. "Oh, you guys are diabolical. No Lillibette, she didn't happen to mention it. Ha! I thought I'd already heard the closer."

Lillibette looked a little confused. "You know May got it all fixed up as three units and one of the units has come up empty for January. Mama hates it when any of the units are empty in the winter. If there's a freeze, the pipes could burst if there's no one there to drip the faucets. You'd be helping us out."

I shot a look at Mom. "And there it is - guilt. The kicker."

Lillibette seemed baffled. I even wondered if I'd gotten it wrong - was she not in cahoots with them? Then... "No guilt. Just a bee for---"

Mom suddenly laughed. "For your bonnet!" I laughed too. Then Lillibette.

I gave Mom the shame-shame fingers. "There's

an old Jewish saying, 'If ten men tell you you're drunk, lie down.' I'm hearing what you're saying. You want me to think about it and I will. I will think about it, but Mom, you heard what I said. I've got insurance and a pension to think about."

Lillibette jumped in. "I hear there's a lot of work down here."

"So I've heard. But it's a completely different market and the timing is potentially disastrous for my career."

Mom gave me the pshaw hand. "Is that all?"

We laughed. But I did think about it. I thought about it as I stayed at Ava's visiting with my family, feeling at peace and surrounded by love. I thought about it when Lillibette and I went into the city for a day and walked around the French Quarter. We tried out a couple of balcony bars and restaurants and enjoyed watching the alcohol-infused chaos below. We danced at a bar on Bourbon at three in the afternoon. We checked out racks and racks of Saints shirts on Decatur and found plenty of cute ones to ooh and ahh over. We walked past a guy frozen in a wide-stanced mid-stride wearing a white suit and red, white and blue top hat. He was holding the leash of a tiny toy dog frozen in tugging him along. We stopped and listened to a brass band playing in front of the Foot Locker wall. They were kids between fifteen and twenty-something and they were so dang good.

When I called to wish Sofia a happy New Year's Eve's Eve, I told her what I'd been thinking. I told her about the practical considerations and I told her about the people here and the food and the music. I told her it was true that the new tax incentives here had created more work but the good parts would still be cast out of L.A. I told her that I'd always had a fantasy of living in the city but that I'd only made a plan for living on the river. Then I told her about the room in the family house.

"Wait, what? You have a rent-free room for a month? In the city?"

"The Garden District. If New Orleans had a Beverly Hills, that would probably be it. They have a private police force like Beverly Hills. And gorgeous old manor homes."

"You have to stay."

I laughed. "Marilyn is pretty dang sure I have to go. She's a pit bull when she gets her teeth in something and she's convinced the dress thing is---"

Sofia made a rare interruption. "The secret to life is knowing what to say yes to."

"Don't I say yes to my career taking off? Do I say yes to some fantasy about living in New Orleans when I'm finally having another moment in L.A.?"

"Um, yeah. That's why the room opened up just when you needed it."

"I don't need it. It would just be fun."

"What are you doing for New Year's?"

"Going with my cousin to watch a concert then see fireworks on the river."

Sofia dropped the phone then picked it up again. "What'd you do last year?"

"Came here."

"Charlotte, I just spilled olive oil on the kitchen floor and the cat's looking interested. I gotta go. Happy New Year. Say yes."

And she was gone.

Chapter 8

I was still thinking about it - staying for a month, but I'd pretty much resigned myself to being responsible and practical and grateful for my rare privilege of doing something I love for money. My cousins and I had spent the afternoon having drinks in different bars throughout the French Quarter. I liked Lafitte's Blacksmith Shop. It was a smelly old bar with a giant two-sided brick fireplace in the middle and sooted brick walls. The bar was entirely candlelit and was the oldest continuous bar in the United States. Despite Lady Gaga's *Poker Face* playing on the jukebox and the Saints-shirt-wearing patrons, the place easily transported me to the late 1700's when the pirate Jean Lafitte would clank tankards with his band of raiders here. I could see their slouchy boots, their sea-faring beards, their wide belts with hand-tooled buckles. After Lafitte helped Jackson defeat the British in the Battle of New Orleans, he and his band of brothers were pardoned and celebrated in this bar.

That battle might have been the last time the city was this united in one cause. A motley crew of local army regulars, militia men, free men of color, Native Americans, New Orleans' elite and the pirates all joined forces and demolished the shocked British troops. I wondered if they had their own "Here we come to get you" type song.

As midnight drew near, my cousins bought two twelve-packs of beer from the Rouses and headed out to Jackson Square for the free concert. I wasn't sure who the Ying Yang Twins were but everyone seemed pretty excited to see them take the stage. It wasn't until I heard those ominous horns that I understood why. EVERYONE sang along, "Stand up and get crunk!" I looked around at our motley mix of people. Their faces were full of passion and optimism and pride. It was beautiful.

I leaned into Lillibette's ear. "When is the Super Bowl?"

She shouted back. "February. But Krewe du Vieux is the end of January. It's the satire parade. The one with all of the penises and Nagin jokes. And the playoffs start in a couple weeks."

I thought about that.

We danced and shouted Who Dats and partied like it was 1999. We stopped on the hill next to the Jax Brewery and watched the Baby Bacchus drop at midnight. Then we found a spot along the river and watched the dueling fireworks shot from barges. I looked out to the Crescent City Bridge spanning the Mississippi. I watched fireworks explode and light the faces of my cousins. I saw the buildings and landmarks on the river's edge all glowing in bursts.

I realized in a flash that I would regret missing this opportunity to stay in my family home for a month in my favorite city in the world - for free. What was the point of working ridiculously hard for eight years if you couldn't take a vacation after? If I'd won it in some karmic raffle, no one would argue with me collecting the prize, would they?

Maybe I'd just lost faith in my career "moments" playing out in the way I'd hoped. It was true that each of those moments pushed my career further, kept me in the game longer, but there was always something that stopped them from reaching their potential. So much had gone sideways between the day we came up with the movie idea and the night of the premiere. The critics hated our film. And a dress was just a dress at the end of the day. Maybe I just realized that if this is what it felt like for my dreams to come true, maybe I needed new dreams.

I was fairly certain either decision could lead to regret. I'd come to forks in the road like this before. I just needed to figure out which regret would mean more to me. My rule was that the secret to life was knowing what to yes to and the way to know what to say yes to was to choose the path that took you closer to your goal. This time was different. This last series of disappointments, betrayals and heartbreaks was longer and rougher than the others. It didn't just level me emotionally and financially, cost me attending weddings and funerals and adversely affect my relationships, it dipped me into the darkness of clinical depression. I was beginning to wonder if my goal of being a working actor and contributing to film history was interfering with my goal of being happy. I needed to figure out which goal meant the most to me.

Which is what I explained to Sofia when I called her later that night.

Sofia unexpectedly laughed. "You think too much. You're just staying for a month. It's not like you're throwing your career out the window to work at McDonald's in New Orleans. Don't you always say that if you want to get acting work, you should plan a vacation?"

"That's true. It's like washing your car to make it rain. You know what's crazy? The thing I can't stop thinking about is how stupid it would be to miss the next football game."

"Seriously?"

I tried to think of the right words. "There's something happening here. There's a feeling happening here right now. I can't describe it. That's why I can't leave because it won't matter if I watch the game on TV in L.A. and read all the articles about what it was like to be in New Orleans that day, no one will be able to make me feel it. I don't know if I can live with that."

"Do that thing your mom says. Flip a coin to see what you really want."

I looked around. "I don't have a coin handy."

"Okay, pick a hand."

I closed my eyes. "Alright, uh, right."

"Come back to L.A. Quick! How do you feel? Did you go 'Yay!' or 'Oh?'"

"Oh."

"And that's that. You're staying and watching that game."

"Yay!"

Chapter 9

Lillibette and I pulled up in front of the family home in the Garden District. My great-grandparents had it built in the late 1800's after the war. Maw Maw grew up in this house then raised my mother here. The building didn't have showy columns or a wide front porch but it was quietly elegant.

It was weird walking past the front door and taking the narrow stone path toward the back of the house. The new slicing and dicing of the home had separated a lone fireplace with a tall, regal staircase. Simple stained glass windows climbed with the stairs. When we reached the landing there were two doors. Lillibette selected a key and inserted it. "Voila."

It was so strange seeing these familiar spaces repurposed. My bedroom would be the old sitting room with the giant bay window area and a fireplace. The back staircase had been closed off from the lower floor and the resulting narrow hallway had been converted to a closet. The back porch was now enclosed and made over as the kitchen and living area. Though the place was bare, the previous tenants had left their synthetic Christmas tree. I looked out the back window. The carriage house was falling apart but it grounded me in childhood memories when this place was intact.

I was standing on the back porch as a teenager, looking out at the magnolia tree and head-high azaleas lining the property. I was a seven-year-old climbing to the hay loft in the carriage house and collecting horseshoes, rusty nails and buttons. I was a tot sitting on the horses' grave under the magnolia tree. I was a gangly kid and Paw Paw was sipping a sweet tea and telling me that Tex was a sturdy horse who'd made the journey from Texas to New Orleans then promptly passed. Then I was a middle-aged woman looking out a kitchen window.

Taffy arrived and we followed Lillibette down the spiral staircase to the carriage house to gather the air mattress, a card table, two foldout wood-slatted deck chairs and a bunch of plastic milk crates. Lillibette smiled when she saw the bag reading "Krewe of Endymion" and grabbed it too. It took several trips around the front of the house and up the tall staircase inside but there was no way some of those items were going up a spiral. We set up the air mattress and unfolded the table and chairs. Lillibette unzipped the Endymion bag and pulled out a handful of beads and a purple plastic Frisbee. "For your tree."

Taffy smiled. "Yes!"

I was lost.

"Your Mardi Gras tree! After Christmas, you redecorate the tree for Carnival."

"Seriously?"

"You'll get more beads and stuff if you stay for Mardi Gras but there's some fun things in here." She pulled out a stack of plastic go-cups with krewe logos, a bracelet made of shiny stilettos crowded like bananas, a purple, green and gold-spiraled football and a crawfish plush-toy. "It'll be fun, give you somethin' to do after I leave." She looked down at the phone she'd just pulled from her silk purse. "Which is now! Gotta go. Taffy, you can get home okay? I was going to give you a ride—"

Taffy waved her off. "Do you. I'll stay and help with the sheets."

"Later gators!" Lillibette grabbed her go-cup and headed for the door.

Taffy and I smiled at each other then laughed together. Taffy headed down the hall. "Let's get those sheets done."

"I know this is Maw Maw's house but it feels so different. Only this room and the smell when you first walk in are the same."

Taffy pointed. "And that wonky bathroom with the tilted tub."

I hadn't remembered the tilted floor with the door cut to match until she said it. "Oh right, and there's no plugs in there. Damn."

"Nope. Get yourself an extension cord. Run it down the hall." She shook a fitted sheet out and pulled a corner down over the air mattress and I did the same. We were already on the pillows when she looked at me and paused. "I need a favor."

That stopped me. I was surprised I might be of any real use to her.

"Mama made us swear to keep that chandelier hung in the family home."

"Right, in her will."

"It's more than just the will, it's our whole lives. That and earnin' college when your uncle said he'd pay if we got good enough grades in high school. It's the only two promises she ever demanded from us. Anyway, I can't really take it back home with me in the two-seater and my sister's place has eight foot ceilings."

"Can't Chiffon store it at her place?"

"Mama always said it has to hang. It can't just sit on the ground somewhere. So I was thinkin' maybe you could hang it here. This isn't exactly the family home but she cleaned it and cared for it nearly her whole life. Mama Heck died in this house."

"Really? Why, was she visiting Sassy?"

"Naw, she was working for your Maw Maw's mama."

"Wait. Mama Heck is the one that helped raise Maw Maw? I didn't know that. I though they found your mother at a bus stop." My head was swimming.

"They did. They were on the way to buy dresses, I think the story goes, and they spotted Mama at the bus stop and your Maw Maw thought she recognized her and called her over."

"So, Ava knew who she was too?"

"I don't know. Mama Heck quit bringin' her and UncaParis around when they got old enough to go to school. It had to be at least ten years of growin' they both did. And Mama was a few years older than your aunt so she might not even have been born yet when Mama went off to school."

"That's so wild. I had no idea." I liked the idea that Taffy's family and mine had been growing up together for three generations. As a child of divorce and a practical person with a dreamer's life, I was always looking for anchors to cling to, signs of continuity.

"So can you hang it here? The chandelier?"

I looked up at the medallion centered in the high ceiling. Wires dangled from it. "This is where Ava had the one she's got hanging in her foyer now. Do you know how to connect it?"

"UncaParis'll come do it. He already said so." She stood holding the half-dressed pillow.

"I guess so. Why not, right?"

Taffy looked up to the ceiling, "Thank you, Jesus." Her head dropped and she smiled at me. "Thank you, Charlotte."

My memory snapped. "Taffy, is that your real name?"

She went back to covering pillows. "Short for Taffeta."

"Like the fabric? Wait Taffeta and Chiffon? Like the fabrics?"

"Yeah, I guess. I always thought Chiffon was like the pie I guess. Mama always said she was sweet as pie."

Now I had to know. "What's your full name?"

She laughed and threw a pillow down on the air mattress. "Always with the questions. Azure Taffeta."

"And your sister?"

"Violet Chiffon."

"Not Lemon? Lemon would make more sense if it was for pie. What if those were fabrics in the laundry basket you guys were in when she first met you?"

Now she really laughed. "I seriously doubt anyone ever brought taffeta and chiffon to that beat-up old place."

I thought about that. "Right. You're probably

right."

"You probably right too, in a way. She probably just picked the prettiest fabrics she could think of."

"Maybe."

"We decided to go ahead and look for her, the lady what birthed us. UncaParis ain't havin' it. He says only a witchy woman would do her kids like that. He said to drop it 'fore anyone gets hurt, let sleepin' dogs lie."

I unfolded a quilt. "He might have a point."

"Maybe so, but he knows who his mama and papa is so he can't know this pain."

"Fair enough."

She motioned to the room. "I think you got this. I'm gonna try to get the streetcar before it gets dark. They say rain later. I wanna beat it home."

The apartment was too quiet with everyone gone. I opened my laptop and danced a little to songs by Snoop Dogg, Notorious B.I.G., Tom Tom Club and Earth, Wind and Fire as I unpacked clothes into a stack of milk crates. I looked up to the ceiling medallion to picture Sassy's chandelier hanging there and dropped the J Brand jeans in my hand. The wires that had been dangling above us were tied neatly in a bow. "What the hell!?!" My voice echoed a little.

I looked around. I rewound every moment we'd been in this room. Then I ran down the hall to the living room and texted Taffy. "Did you look at the wires in the ceiling medallion?" I was aware it was a weird question and I wasn't much for this whole texting thing but I already knew my mind wouldn't rest.

She texted back. "What? Yes I guess."

I stared at my phone's keypad. "Can you describe how they looked?"

I waited minutes that felt long before she finally replied. "Some black wires. Maybe a green one?"

I had a rule. If it took more than three texts, it was easier to call. But I felt pretty confident about this next question. "Were they tied in any way?"

She got back to me immediately this time. "Hanging."

I didn't know how to sort out all the thoughts in my brain. There was a collision between my understanding of physics and the way the world works and the reality that we'd both seen dangling wires and now they were tied in a bow. Taffy texted to ask why I'd asked about the wires but I texted I'd tell her later. I dialed Sofia.

"Hey! How's the house? Did you move in?"

"It's great. There's something really cool about being in the house I came to all my life. It's weird, though, not being able to go into the rest of the house. I can't even go through the front door anymore."

"Ew, I wouldn't like that."

I pulled at one of the fake branches on my new faux foliage. "I got a tree. The last people left their synthetic Christmas tree here and my cousin gave me some beads and toys and stuff to decorate it for Mardi Gras."

"Fun! Put a picture on Facebook when you're done."

"I don't—"

"I forgot, you don't do Facebook. You have to do something. You're going to be there a whole month. You should start a blog."

I laughed. "That's what you always say."

Then she laughed. "What if I'm always right?"

"Fair enough. But it was such a drag when I did that other one."

She laughed louder. "It was about Katrina. Of course it was a drag. Plus you were doing it because someone else made you."

"You mean like you're making me now?"

Sofia got more serious. "You're always saying a picture's worth a thousand words and you keep saying you wish I was there - so put me there. Take pictures and tell me what you experienced. You don't have to say who you are or anything personal, just say what happened."

It seemed like a lot of work. But then, I didn't have much work to do while I was here. "I'll think about it."

"Just do it."

I looked at the pile of indescribable toys, beads and goodies on the floor. "I promise I'll take a picture of the tree and somehow, you'll see it."

Satisfied, she moved on. "So you like the unit?"

"No, it's great. It's perfect but Sofia, the weirdest thing happened."

"Bad weird or good weird?"

That was the question. "There were these wires hanging down from the ceiling when we went into the bedroom and after Taffy left, I looked up and they were tied in a bow."

"What? No. Run. No. No way."

I laughed. "I know, I know. You get creeped out easy. It's not, like, scary per se, but it was... unsettling."

"It would unsettle me right out of that house and back to my aunt's."

"But there has to be some explanation."

Sofia nearly shouted. "Spirits not at rest! That's the explanation."

"Honestly, I haven't been able to come up with a better one." Not yet, anyway.

Her voice sounded intense. "What were you talking about when it happened?"

"I don't know, we talked about hanging the chandelier. Oh and Taffy's name. The twins were named for fabrics. We were talking about that."

Sofia was quiet a moment. "Where does the chandelier go?"

"We're going to connect it to those wires."

"Ghost. Totally a ghost."

I laughed. "Fine. I have a roommate." I laughed some more but my mind was chasing thoughts.

Chapter 10

I'd never had a fake tree before but it was easy to see some of the advantages. Not only would I not have to water it, but I could have left it up from Thanksgiving to Mardi Gras without it dying. Plus, the branches would bend to my will so I could more perfectly space the beads and other parade throws. But it was clear this quarter-full bag wasn't going to be enough to decorate and I wondered if you could still find lights this time of year. It was as good an excuse as any to take a walk in the neighborhood.

I found my way to Magazine Street and followed it uptown. Even in winter, the live oaks filled the skyline like a convoluted canopy of branches over the passing cars and bikes. I passed grand old manor homes and younger century-old houses - all decked in Saints decorations. Some homes still had their Christmas bows and wreaths up, but even those shared space with Who Dat Nation flags of black and gold stripes with fifty fleur de lis for stars. "I Believe" and "Bless Our Boys" signs were taped in the windows. I even saw an inflated snowman wearing a Saints helmet.

When I reached the shops and restaurants, I spotted an older man with long salt-n-pepper dreadlocks. As I drew closer, I could see he had a milky eye. He smiled at me and I lit up from inside.

"Hey."

"Hey. It's a beautiful day. Have a blessed day." He watched me pass.

"You too!" I never had enough of these moments in L.A. People spent a lot of their time in cars there. So I drank in that feeling of connecting with people and feeling the goodness in them. Though he had smelled freshly bathed, I made the assumption dreadlocks-guy was a man of the streets.

I peeked in the windows I passed finding fun collections of vintage toys, hand-crafted jewelry and Who Dat gear. I looked around the Walgreen's for tree lights and left with their last two strands as well as glitter, glue and glossy school folders in purple, green and gold - the colors of Mardi Gras.

When I exited the store, the man with the dreadlocks was sitting at the display chair in front of the interior design store across the street. He waved to me, his other arm resting on the white display table next to a "SALE" placard. I waved back. In L.A., I was always baffled that the churches fenced off their stoops at night so the homeless wouldn't sleep there. I hoped the folks at Design Within Reach were more compassionate.

Back at the house, I cut masks and fleur de lis out of the folders and edged them with contrasting glitter then set them out to dry while I hung the lights around the tree and strung plastic-beaded necklaces from branch to branch. My homemade ornaments caught the light and sparkled among the plush-toys, foam footballs and plastic cups. I couldn't wait for it to get dark.

We found out the doorbell didn't work for this

unit when Taffy and Paris stood outside for far too long holding the chandelier before finally getting me by phone. When Paris headed out the back to get a ladder from the carriage house, Taffy grabbed my wrist. "Chiffon and I been talkin' and we got somethin' to ask you."

"Sure, sure." I became suddenly nervous.

"You so good at questions and thinkin' things out. We was hopin' you'd help us find our other mother."

Now I knew why I was nervous. I'd seen it coming the minute she clutched my arm. I was going to have to disappoint her. "I'd have no idea how to do that. I wouldn't even know where to begin."

"Yeah, but you know what to ask. All you gotta figure out is who to ask."

I thought about that. "But I don't know anyone. Y'all know who to ask better than I ever could."

"Honestly Charlotte, we been thinkin' about this a long time and hadn't come up with one thing yet. You can't do any worse."

We heard Paris clanking against the doorframe and walking down the hall adjusting the metal ladder in his grip. Taffy shot me a look. "Don't say nothin'."

I nodded as Paris set the ladder up under the medallion and untied the wire bow. "Taffy, fetch me a cuppa water."

Taffy said, "Yes sir" as I said, "I can get it."

Paris nodded to Taffy. After she left, he turned his gaze to me. "Not sure this would pass muster with Cassandra. Seems like y'all tryin' to get away wit' somethin'. People beyond the grave, they see all. They know whatchu up to."

Taffy handed him a go-cup of water. "Leave her

be, UncaParis." I wondered if she'd gotten the cup from the tree or found where I'd stored the rest in the cabinet. She gestured to me. "Charlotte got enough problems with spirits without you stirrin' the pot."

I sat down near the blanket-bundled chandelier and worked at the knots in the ropes. Paris came down from the ladder and handed Taffy the empty cup. "People need to know when to leave things be."

Taffy reverted to sassing. "You ain't even talkin' about the damn chandelier anymore. I done told you already that Mama said we can't betray her. Who're you to doubt her wisdom?"

He was yelling now. "No good can come from finding trash. Only a fool wastes one minute on trash. She threw you away like trash and that's what that bitch is, born trash and gonna die trash."

I freed the ropes and pulled back the blanket revealing the familiar heirloom. It really was beautiful, intricate and elaborate without being busy and cluttered. I thought I heard once that it was from Paris. I touched some of the cut crystals as Taffy and her uncle yelled about trash and betrayal. They were both right so this could take awhile. I ran my finger up to the crystal-encrusted fixture at the top. There was a small piece of yellowed masking tape hanging off the edge.

I scooted around on the wooden floor to better see the top. Two pieces of old tape were placed sloppily around the brass rim. I pulled one slowly up wondering if I was doing something the family wouldn't like - if they noticed I was still here. There was a small inscription. I had to stare at it a long time before I could make anything of it. It looked like

"LW DW," but the fancy script was scratched into weathered and tarnished brass so it was hard to tell. Maybe it was "SW OW." Definitely letters, maybe initials?

Paris and Taffy kept on about damnation and regrets while I pulled the other piece of tape. I was pretty sure I was being bad, maybe even destroying property, but I couldn't resist. The finely imprinted stamp was much easier to see but I wasn't sure what it was. Definitely a symbol of some sort but I wasn't even sure what was the top and what was the bottom. A long, funny watering can? Some kind of weird rifle? An instrument? I felt like I'd seen it somewhere before but I truly couldn't place it. I wished I could take a photo but the fight was winding down and I started to worry they'd notice the tape.

Paris demanded, "Let's get this thing hung and get on outa here. Leave this woman be. She don't need to know our bizness." I started to say it was fine but he turned his back and headed up the ladder.

Taffy winked at me when they left.

I went to the back of the house and the tree looked beautiful in the dark. I'd take photos when it got light out again. My busy brain replayed the evening. Could I help the twins find their other mother? Where would I start? Did it mean anything that Paris called her a bitch like he knew her? Was he protecting the twins from a woman he knew to be trash? Wait, was he their dad? How better to know if someone is trash than to be the one she was trashy with?

Down the hall, I heard the tinkling of glass. I waited for it to happen again.

Was the whole laundry story even true? It was a crazy story like the stork bringing babies, the kind of thing you tell a kid when something's too difficult to explain. But that would have to mean the real story was even lower than giving your kids to a stranger in a laundromat. Not likely. Even finding out your uncle is really your father who asked his sister to raise you would have been easier to handle. Unless he raped the woman. No. Sassy wouldn't let him around the girls if that were the case. But maybe he knew the other mother. Maybe they were a couple and she cheated on Paris. Ha! That could be it. Maybe I would start with asking Paris... And then he'd yell for hours.

The glass tinkling happened again.

I got up from the foldout chair and made my way down the long, dark hall. I turned on the light-switch in the bedroom and the chandelier glowed brightly. It was beautiful. It was also moving. The dangling bits beneath were swaying like someone had gently run a stick across them. A truck rolled by half a block away and the house wiggled a bit in the gelatinous earth. "Truck. That's it."

Though I couldn't help but notice it didn't make the noise this time.

Chapter 11

I awoke to rainbows dancing on the walls and looked up at the chandelier hanging above the air mattress. Beautiful. It was getting easier to believe someone would drag this chandelier from Texas to New Orleans before cars were king. I padded in sock-feet down the hall and smiled at my Mardi Gras tree.

I wasn't entirely sure how to spend my days this month but I shoved a pad of paper and a pen into one of my hand-crocheted backpacks, the black and grey one with the feathery black trim on top. It wasn't black and gold but it would have to do.

It was cold out, too cold. Mom always said we were hothouse flowers (people who needed heat and humidity) so forty degrees felt brutal. But, I walked to the corner of St. Charles and stood waiting under wind-blown live oaks still littered with last year's Mardi Gras beads.

Most of the people on the streetcar seemed to be tourists. Some were clearly from climates where this cold snap was t-shirt weather - long-sleeved. Other riders were clearly locals, people in hotel uniforms, restaurant uniforms and other black-pant-sensible-shoe jobs. One guy stood with a guitar case leaning against his leg and a kid sat with a trumpet on his lap.

I got off at Canal and bristled against the cold. This was a terrible idea. L.A. may have been more like a brittle, dry sauna than a muggy hothouse, but it was almost never this cold there in the daytime and not often at night either. This sucked. I was certainly going to have to abandon any fantasies of finding a balcony today. Walking down Royal in search of a warm bar or coffee shop, I peered in the shop windows. Some were virtually unchanged from my childhood like the Civil War shop with plain, white window wells stocked with guns and coins.

When I first heard the violin down the street, it sounded like heaven calling. As I got closer, I saw it was the duet from Cafe du Monde playing *Freebird*. One audience member held up a lighter. The others held up cell phones. I pulled my jacket tighter and stood for awhile watching. Sometimes, I closed my eyes and just listened. And swayed. When the song sped up, I opened them and realized the guy next to me was watching me. He smiled a little. "They're amazing, right?"

"Yes." I smiled back - a little.

He laughed a little. "Yeah, you right. You were gettin' into it."

"I was just thinking I wish my friend was here to hear this. She'd love this."

"Where's your friend?"

"In L.A."

"The other LA."

My turn to laugh a little. "Yes, Los Angeles, not Louisiana."

"Is that your phone?"

"What?"

"Is that your phone ringing?"

Startled, I struggled to get my backpack off over

my sweater-filled jacket. I dug around frantically before my fingers finally found the phone and pushed "talk."

Marilyn sounded giddy. "Do you have a pen?"

I struggled to pull out the note pad and the smiling guy grabbed my bag to help me. I uncapped the pen. "Shoot."

"You got the job! The director loved you."

"Really?" And that's why you never know until you know. And even then, anything can happen. A career in acting is an exercise in surrendering to the unknown. Marilyn gave me the details and I scribbled them all down. One day of work next week and they needed me to be able to shoot a gun. For real. I was confused. "None of this was in the sides I got."

"Right. They gave that part to Laura Linney. But the director loved you so much they wrote a part for you."

"Does it involve underwear?" I smiled weakly at the guy holding my backpack.

"I think you change clothes at some point. It's a small part but it's good. You'll like it."

I thanked her, hung up and dumped everything into the backpack. The guy held it up by the straps and offered it to me. "I gotta ask. Does what involve underwear?"

I shook my head. "Ugh. It's an acting job."

"In a play?"

"A movie." I never knew how much to say in these situations.

"You just got a job in a movie? We've gotta celebrate! Come on, lemme buy you a drink."

I took him in. Warm smile and kind eyes, light

hair greying at the temples, black wool coat and bright green gloves.

"I could go for a hot chocolate."

He held the door open for me at a nearby restaurant and we took two stools at the bar. He ordered for us then excused himself. I hated this part, the part where I wasn't sure if this guy was just being nice or if this was some fantasy of his that he could get me in bed over a mug of hot chocolate. A brass band passed by the windows followed by a bride and groom and their wedding party.

The guy returned and took a sip of his Irish Coffee. "Oh, that's good." He nodded to the bartender. "Outstanding." Then he lifted his glass to me. "To getting the underwear job."

I laughed. "To getting the underwear job." I hoped he wasn't one of those guys who always wants you to be a good sport.

"Did you come here for work?"

"Family funeral. The timing just worked out well."

He lifted his glass again. "To good timing." We clicked glasses and took sips. "And families in New Orleans." He clicked my glass again and took another sip. That was it, he was a drinker. "Were you born here? I know you didn't go to school here or I'd've foundya."

I gave him the spiel, how my parents met at LSU and moved on their honeymoon. How I wasn't really from here but if home is where the heart is, this is my heart's home. I think he gave me partial credit. He told me about the bar we were sitting in and introduced me to the bartender, Bradley, who'd been working there since he was a teenager - just like his father and grandfather had before him. In L.A., most of the people who worked in restaurants wouldn't admit it was their job much less their career. I loved the idea of three generations standing behind the same bar pouring drinks for regulars and tourists, collecting stories and taking pride in their work. I always tried to take pride in my work, even when the job involved a plastic name-tag or plunging toilets. I loved how my values made sense here.

Then the guy stood, downed his drink and extended his hand. "Duty calls. Congratulations on the job. Bradley, take care of this one. I'm headin' out. Who Dat!"

Bradley spun his bar rag in the air, "Who Dat, baby!" He looked to my mug. "You want a warm up?"

"I'm good. Do you mind if I sit here awhile, write a few things down?"

Bradley the bartender let me be for awhile while I wrote notes like, "MG tree, violinist and guitarist, bartender - Bradley." I looked around for the name of the place. I had to admit I had the buy-you-a-drink guy all wrong. He never even tried to exchange names much less bodily fluids. He was that rare breed - a gentleman. Or married. Maybe he was just a nice married guy who didn't want to drink alone. Which would still make him a gentleman. Bradley seemed to have the whole gentleman thing on lockdown as well.

"You need somethin'?"

"I was looking for the name of this place."

He slid me a book of matches. "You writin' a

book? Lotsa folks come here to write books. Seems to inspire 'em." He nodded toward a mule pulling a Who Dat-decorated carriage past the windows.

"I'm thinking of starting a blog." I could see that meant nothing to him. "It's like an online journal, like a series of articles but you don't usually have an editor. It's just your thoughts on something. Mine would have photos."

"Of New Orleans?"

"Of the stuff I notice. The stuff I love about here. It's for a friend of mine."

He wiped glasses dry and stacked them. "Sounds like a lot of work just for one reader."

"Yeah. But she's a really good friend. But, like, do you know this city is unique? Have you been other places?"

He looked around. "Who needs it? I've got this."

Such a simple thought. I was raised thinking thoughts like that. Then I spent decades surrounded by people who always wanted more. I wasn't even sure I knew what I wanted anymore but I knew it didn't involve half-million-dollar cars and private planes (although I had to admit I was a fan of the G4 and it didn't suck to skip security and have the plane take off when you got there).

When I got home, I plugged the tree in and took a few photos. I framed some full-length then took close-ups of ornaments. I uploaded the photos while I ate the dinner I'd brought home from the bar. Red beans and rice with greens.

I should've remembered to bring my camera to the French Quarter. I'd already told Sofia about the violinist and guitarist so without photos, it seemed a bit pointless to mention musicians Sofia wouldn't be able to hear. Maybe I'd skip the bar and Bradley, too. Just focus on the tree.

I found a free site to build the blog and set up a simple template as my "home page." All I needed was a name. I jotted a few ideas on my notepad then typed ideas into the template to see how they looked. I said my favorite out loud to hear how it sounded, "LA to NOLA." Settled.

Cricket noises announced a text message from Taffy. "You in?"

Was I? I wasn't being modest, I really had no idea where to start looking for their other mother. There was Paris but it seemed fairly clear he was in no mood to be helpful. There were the twins' names but I was willing to take it fairly literally that the meaning Sassy had given them was that they were named for pretty fabric, that they were better than what they'd come from - more fine. That was probably all that it was. If they ever did find their other mother and she did turn out to be trash, of course Sassy would want them to remember they were better than that.

I dialed her. "Hey Taffy. I really don't see how I can help. I thought maybe your names were a clue but I'm kind of off of that now. I think they're just beautiful names for beautiful girls. And you're uncle's not havin' it."

"Forget UncaParis. He always thought Mama was crazy for takin' us on in the first place. Don't say no. Just think on it. You don't have to do anything, just keep thinkin' on it, ya heard me? Maybe you come up with somethin'."

If I couldn't find the woman, the least I could do is not interfere with the twins' hope. "I can do that."

Taffy exhaled and I realized she'd been holding her breath. "Thank you. Thank, you Charlotte. You can't know."

I laughed nervously. "I'm not saying I can find her. I don't really know how to do that. But I promise I'll think about it."

"That's all we askin'."

"I can do that."

Chapter 12

I'd held fake guns before. As kids, my brother and I played cops and robbers with cap guns. Sofia and her sister and I once made a funny video, a spoof of *Charlie's Angels* where we used brightly colored plastic squirt guns. And I'd carried and even pointed prop guns on movie sets. But so far, I'd never fired a prop gun (though I had gotten "shot" a couple times).

The scariest thing about holding the real-life Glock 9 was that a mistake could result in death. In movies, there was almost always a second take. I'd be lying if I said I wasn't scared. I'd heard a lot about kickback and worried about my long, gangly arms and my low bodyweight. What if it knocked me back and the gun went off again? A real bullet would be in the room with us. Anything could happen.

The pleasantly authoritative employee behind me said calmly, "Now, stay relaxed, breathe in and gently pull the trigger back. You won't need to squeeze hard. Ready?" He snapped his ear muffs down.

"I really hope so."

"You'll be fine. Don't tell anyone I said this but women are generally better at this. Especially at first. No need to be a nervous Nelly. You've got the advantage."

I thought about that. Then I took a breath and gently squeezed the trigger on the exhale. HOLY

SHIT! That was loud. That was terrifying. That was so brutal and final.

The man slapped his gloves together. "Whoa Nelly! What'd I tell you? Look what you did."

I'd forgotten to see if I actually hit the target. The hole was at the nine o'clock position of the bullseye on the outline's chest. "That's pretty good."

"Pretty good? Little lady, you just hit the bullseye first time out. Let's see if it's just beginner's luck. Check your grip. Aim up. Relax. And breathe."

BAM! A few inches to the upper right of the bullseye. BAM! Four inches down. I'd overcompensated. BAM! Bullseye.

The guy laughed. "Damn girl. Don't piss you off, right?"

I guess I understood why so many people said they feel power when they shoot a gun but I couldn't help but feel totally aware that we were laughing and having fun but one twitch could end us. But, I had to admit it felt really good to be good at it. I felt a little more "alpha," more post-apocalyptic.

I was still feeling that way when I got home and called Marilyn to tell her I'd gone to the gun range and rocked it.

"That's awesome. I knew you would be good at this. I knew it! You can do anything."

I laughed. "I don't know about that but I can play it on TV and that's gonna have to do."

Marilyn deadpanned, "I've been thinking, you should try to get an agent while you're down there."

"Are you serious? I'm only going to be here a few more weeks. Who's going to take an actor who doesn't live here?"

She laughed. "I'm thinking all of them. You're a big fish in a small pond down there. Someone's going to be willing to give it a shot if they think they might make some money."

She had a point. "But, still. Marilyn, it's kinda ridiculous."

Her voice got sharper. "No, what's ridiculous is you being there for the last breaths of this dress moment. But I agreed to that---"

"And it turned out great! I got a job out of it so I wasn't totally crazy." Wait, did I just make her point?

"Right. And you may as well use your time there. They don't know from dress moments but there's work down there right now. I'm seeing it all the time on the Breakdowns."

"Anything you pay attention to, you're going to see a lot of." I wasn't sure why I was arguing against this. I loved working. I didn't have an agent in L.A., just my manager, Marilyn. And she was asking for a little help. And helping her was a win-win situation. "Fine. I'll do it. I'll send out an email to a few agents. I promise."

"Great. You'll get to meet new agents and casting directors. They'll love you. It'll be great."

"I'm doing it right now. Bye."

It didn't take long on my laptop to find the rather short list of local agents. I opened an old email I'd written in L.A. and updated it then sent it to the agent with the best-by-far client list, Claudia Speicher. I thought about sending it to a few others for safety but decided to give it a day. Based on her taste in actors, I really only wanted to be with Claudia.

I started to close my computer then stopped. I

looked up "laundromat Treme" in Google Maps and found three. I knew Clothespin Laundromat on Rampart was the one that used to be a studio where Jerry Lee Lewis and Ray Charles recorded. The twins were probably born when it was still a recording studio. Then I checked Washing Well Laundryteria. I remembered it on Bourbon in the French Quarter - which seemed like a long haul from the Treme. But further searching revealed that the business was at least sixty-five years old so it was a possibility. So was the reality that the laundromat may have closed years ago or be one of the "ain't der no mo'" things.

The last one was T & D Drycleaning & Laundry. I'd never heard of that one. I clicked it on the list and the map zoomed onto St. Phillip Street next to Armstrong Park, just blocks from Sassy's home. I couldn't find anything about how long it had been open so I zoomed down to street view. It looked pretty old and like maybe it was never very special. Maybe this was the place. The burgundy wall had white hand-block-painted lettering, "CLEANER." The phone number was nailed into the wall below. Both 5's were missing and had been painted in by a less-skilled hand. I clicked the arrow and rounded the virtual corner. The sign on the front read, "Treme Drycleaners & Laundry." Maybe they'd changed ownership recently.

Maybe Taffy knew. Maybe I could've just asked her. And what would it accomplish anyway? They would've both have been walking distance from the laundry but how would knowing which laundry it was help find a nameless, faceless woman who had lived somewhere around there decades ago and didn't want to be found?

I turned on the tree lights and uploaded photos of my shooting targets while writing notes for my blog post on the gun range. I was kinda mad some of the instructor's fairly-stray bullet holes were on the target. I wouldn't bother mentioning it on the blog, but I might be petty enough to mention it on the phone later.

I posted the blog then checked my email before taking a hot bath in the slightly-tilted cast iron tub. There was a reply from Claudia. "Good to hear from you. I'd heard you were in town. Please call tomorrow. I'd love to work with you."

That was easy.

Chapter 13

Claudia had one of voices they don't make two of - all raspy, weathered and bemused. And she was cool. She was no podunk agent blowing smoke and faking her way along. She was the real deal. Except I was used to having to go in and meet with a table full of agents before signing a stack of legal papers (that mostly favored them). So I was a little taken aback when Claudia closed our fun, get-to-know-you talk with, "Okay, so I'll start sending you out right away."

That was super easy.

It was nearly sixty degrees out so it seemed like a good day for a celebratory walk down Magazine. The Christmas decorations and live tree boughs were all gone from the houses lining the road, replaced by more Who Dat gear or early Mardi Gras wreaths.

I'd seen the owner be amazing on a cake decorating show so I considered stopping for a sweet treat from Sucre but got distracted by some cute t-shirts in the Storyville shopwindow. Like many shops and houses in New Orleans, it was long and narrow inside. T-shirt laden shelves lined the walls and t-shirts and onesies emblazoned with local jokes and symbols hung above them on a clothesline.

The image of the water meter lids had become popular since The Storm. I'd been seeing the familiar symbol on everything from coasters to earrings but I wasn't exactly sure why and considered asking the young, bohemian employee behind the counter. I started to walk closer but held back when I realized how intense his conversation was with the pretty and petite customer holding a black "Who Dat Nation" t-shirt.

"Cease and desist? How can you own 'Who Dat?' It's like sayin' you own 'Go team!' They're even comin' for the fleur de lis. The f-in' fleur de lis! That thing's dawn-of-Paris old."

I couldn't help but jump in. "It's actually Egypt-old."

The employee threw his long arms in the air. "That's what I'm saying. Are they going to sue King Tut?"

The customer nodded in agreement. "Lauren over at Fleurty Girl said she got one too."

"A cease and desist? Who the hell do these people think they are?"

The petite woman looked resigned. "The NFL."

"Fucking Goodell."

Now I was totally intrigued. "Wait, the NFL is stopping you from what?"

The employee and customer turned to me and it was like they'd just now realized I was standing there. The employee grabbed the Who Dat t-shirt from the customer. "This. They say we can't use the fleur de lis and that we can't use the phrase 'Who Dat' which my family has been using all my life and which has been around since before dirt."

The customer piled on. "I mean, is the NFL hurting for money? And aren't they supposed to be a non-profit anyway? Yeah, 'cuz we're just rollin' in cash here. We've just had it too good for too long."

"Goodell sucks."

The petite woman put the t-shirt on the counter and pulled out her wallet. "Who Dat."

The employee rung her up. "Who Dat."

Then my phone rang. Embarrassed, I ran out of the shop to answer Lillibette's call. People mostly didn't use cell phones indoors around here.

"Hey cuz. Anders is playin' tonight. I'll pick you up around nine-ish and we'll head over. Oh, did you hear about this whole NFL thing?"

News travels fast. "Yeah, they were just talking about it in the shop I was in when you called."

"Goodell sucks."

I snickered. "That's what I hear."

I'd been to Tipitina's a couple of times through the years. It was barn-cavernous once you got past the gift shop and the bust of Professor Longhair. I knew enough to rub his head as I passed but I wasn't exactly sure why people did it. Anders was already onstage. He was a scruffy, good looking blonde with a guitar strapped across his Who Dat t-shirted chest.

The crowd here was so different than bar crowds in L.A. Only about a third of the people were in their twenties. The guys mostly bopped their heads forward and back while the girls danced. Another third of the crowd was in their thirties or so. They seemed to know a lot of the words to Anders' original songs. What was so different was that about a third of the audience was over forty, many with grey hair - and not just the men. It wasn't uncommon to see an older man in a bar in L.A. but it was downright unusual to see a woman with grey hair and natural lines on her face. I wasn't even close to the oldest woman in the room. Which was wonderful.

And there were more tall people here. I noticed it in Dallas too. At 5'10", I was the shortest in my family so it felt like home to look so many people in the eye. I accidentally stared too long at the young man bopping beside me.

He smiled a pretty smile. "He's so good, right? You've seen him before?"

I smiled back. "No. But, yeah, he's great. The whole band is."

"You're not from here."

It was a statement, not a question. Was I that obvious? "My parents are but I live in L.A. The other LA."

He laughed then shot me that smile again. "That's okay. Anders isn't from here either. Work or play?"

I thought about that. "I have this weird job that even when I'm not working, I'm always kind of working. Like right now, I'm thinking things like could I use this song for a soundtrack? Does the tax incentive program extend to music? Is this a good location? Are they open seven days or are there days where you could shoot into the night? Things like that."

"Wow, that's a lot of thoughts. I was thinkin' of getting another beer. Can I get you somethin'?"

Here we go. "No thank you."

"Don't work too hard." He flashed the smile again.

"Don't drink too hard." I flashed mine.

He nodded at me. "Yes, ma'am."

Right! Ma'am because I'm old enough to have

given birth to him. Why was it so hard to tell the difference between being hit on and being treated with respect here? How much perspective had I lost? What if it was perfectly normal for men to say nice things to women without expecting sex in exchange? I thought maybe the times had just changed a lot since I'd left the East Coast but what if that was only how things were in L.A. and the rest of the world was just as I'd left it?

Lillibette came back from the bar with a plastic cup of Diet Coke for me. "Oh, this is my favorite song. *Louisiana Rain.*" She started swaying her ample hips, her blonde bob swinging back and forth. She sang along about comin' back home again and sad-smiled about not giving a shit about another hurricane.

The crowd cheered. Many presented their drinks like they were offering a toast. There were moments when I felt so filled with happiness that it spilled over as tears. This was another one of those moments. I felt normal here. I felt like I was just myself and like that was plenty.

There had been a lot of moments lately when I wanted to jump in and "act" like a local. I'd even thought of buying a "Who Dat Nation" t-shirt but I didn't feel I'd earned it. But dancing along with this beautiful love song to my favorite city in the world, I felt I'd totally earned the right to sing about comin' back home again. I left the hurricane lyric to the locals.

I was still getting the hang of this whole blogging thing. I knew I should've brought my camera, taken a few photos of the oft-rubbed Fess head and Anders playing with his band. If I really had been scouting movie locations, I would've never left home without the camera.

Back at the house, I decided to work on my movie role instead of blogging. I plugged the tree in, sat at the card table and got back to digging into the world of "Firearms Instructor." Why did she choose this job? Was she good at it? How long had she been doing it? Did she have a death wish? Was she a daredevil? Was she married? Did she have kids? Why would someone give away their children at a laundromat? Did she already have too many children? Was she not cut out for the task of twins? And why wasn't Sassy worried about them running into her in the neighborhood?

Wait, that might be something. Either the laundromat lady lived in the neighborhood and Sassy wasn't worried about the girls ever finding out who she was for some reason or... Or she was moving? She was a tourist? She died? She was someone's visiting relative? No, still too chancy. Sassy wouldn't have wanted to leave too big an opening for an accidental meeting. The woman didn't live here, right? Sassy knew somehow that she wouldn't have to worry that the woman would be around. Which would make it way harder to find her. Damn.

Chapter 14

Once I arrived on the set in nearby Metairie, I was back in my element. I checked in, dropped my set bag in my trailer and headed to hair and make-up. The trailer was a dance of curling irons, makeup brushes and bursts of sweet-smelling sprays. I recognized one of the actors but didn't know his name.

"Charlotte! This is the one I was telling you guys about!" The two-snaps-up hairdresser waved his wand at me. "Mario. We did that indi together - the one where you were in the trunk of the car. Girl, you were such a trooper." He took in his audience - even the actors were interested. His gestures got wilder. "They had this poor girl tied up, mouth gagged, inside the trunk of a car and when they open the trunk, it's fake-raining out so she's basically getting water-boarded."

I laughed. "I wouldn't go that far, but it---"

He waved me off. "Too modest. I'm telling you guys, this girl works hard for the money."

That felt good. "Thanks." And it was nice to see a vaguely familiar face.

The hair and makeup trailer on most any set was like a local bar in the real world. Actors would tell their "bartenders" everything for at least an hour to three hours a day so the hair and makeup people would end up knowing lots of things about lots of people. Much of the sharing was about the actor's feelings during the shoot. They might talk about being scared to do an emotional scene and start divulging their own life stories and why the scene was hard for them, all while someone fastened a hairpiece. They'd try to keep their face still as they revealed that they'd been having an affair with their costar then saw them flirting with someone else on set - all while a makeup artist applied false eyelashes.

I sat in Mario's chair and he threw a smock over me, affixing it behind my neck. "Is this what you're wearing?"

I shook my head. "I think they're going with the tan jumpsuit uniform but there's still talk of jeans and flannel. It wasn't in my trailer yet but either way, it doesn't go over my head, so go nuts."

"Oh good. I was hoping to go with the purple rollers."

I didn't have to look. I already knew they were the ones as wide as Coke cans. I was hoping my hair might be down and sexy but I sensed a ponytail in my future. The trailer returned to the bustling hive of activity, joke-telling and secret-sharing it had been before I entered.

Mario stopped separating my hair and announced to the room, "I'm just saying there's no way he dumped her. She's like a goddess, like a ripe, worldly goddess full of wisdom and sex appeal. No, he screwed up and she dumped him. That's what happened."

The makeup artist with a local accent and a Saints jersey stretched across her ample bosom jumped in.

"He's hit on every girl on this set. Making up for lost time, I guess."

Mario dragged his comb down my scalp to part another section. "Wants to see if he's still got it."

A beautiful young brunette in a figure-fitting green dress entered and checked for an empty chair. The local lady in the Saints jersey blurted. "Spoiler alert! Yes, he does!" Everyone teased her but she stood firm. "What? I think he's hot. He'd hit on my twenty year old niece, but he's hot."

The beautiful brunette made her way through the trailer. "Are we talking about who I think we're talking about? He just told me I wore this well then looked at me like I was in a garter and thigh-highs."

Mario smoothed a section of hair over a plastic roller and took a clamp from the counter. He looked at me in the reflection on the mirror. "Don't think you're off the hook. He may snack on girls but when he wants a meal, he likes a little mileage."

A lot of the men in L.A. didn't make much of an effort to court women. The natural order had been so messed-with there that women competed for a man just because he had an expensive car or a big boat or a TV show or a sports contract. Some competed just to say they slept with that guy. Over time, it could make men lazy at love. In my experience, the bigger the name, the shorter their game.

I introduced myself to the beautiful brunette, Brooke. She was the stand-in and stunt woman for the lead female. I had to note, "You're a very beautiful stunt woman. Have you considered working in front of the camera?"

"I tried. I did the whole thing, moved to L.A. and

everything. I was there for about a year. Now I do stunts, photo double, whatever. I still act sometimes but I can't do that whole L.A. thing."

I was totally intrigued. "Why? What happened in L.A.?"

She kept her head straight while the hairdresser removed pins from her up-do. "It wasn't anything that happened, it was the vibe. It was just raised different, I guess."

The young guy getting his beard tinted chimed in. "They're oversexed."

I literally guffawed. "What?"

Brooke agreed. "It's everywhere. You're drivin' down the street and BOOM - billboard of four women in sheer lingerie draped over a shirtless guy in a chair."

The guy laughed. "And it's an ad for T-Mobile or something."

Brooke laughed too. "Life insurance."

The guy threw her a high-five from his seat. Then he turned his eyes to me. "But seriously, have you been there? It's all they think about there. Every social event, every decision, every purchase is somehow driven by sex. It's really unbalanced. I mean, sex is great and everything but so is Mardi Gras, so's a crawfish boil, so's an amazing concert. Be here now, you know? Not everything is a prelude to a kiss or whatever."

I'd had those thoughts. Many times. But I believed the people who told me I was weird for wanting to get to know someone before deciding to get involved with them. I'd say to them that the men in my life had to at least pass the will-you-drive-me-to-the-airport test. That seemed like a fair bare-minimum. But some people called me old-fashioned or out-of-touch. One group of guys called me "None," because you'd "get none." Others called me "high-maintenance" or "needy" if I expressed any interest in them. It was all very confusing for someone who grew up taking the concept of "making love" literally. I had a healthy respect for the power of sex.

That said, I'd become so accustomed to the billboards and "hot chicks" in labia-skimming cocktail dresses and six inch Lucite pumps that I hardly noticed them anymore. Heck, some of my dearest friends dressed "for success." And weren't there photos of me all over the web hiding my disappointment by revealing my body?

It was a pretty great day at work. In my experience, movie sets were magical places where people bonded quickly in hopes of making something great. Even one day could feel like a month at summer camp full of private jokes and exchanges of let's-stay-in-touch. For the actors, there's the added bonus of the "work wrap." Whenever an actor finishes a job, even if it's only a one day job, everyone briefly stops what they're doing and claps for them. It doesn't suck.

Even with that nice send-off, I was always sad when a job ended. I didn't have that thing a lot of actors have where they fear they'll never work again, but I never knew when I'd find my way back to a set. It could be tough sometimes - the not knowing.

I couldn't really blog about being on the set. I'd signed a non-disclosure agreement before they'd even give me my four pages of script. I never did see the whole script. That was a first.

I plugged the tree in and opened my lap top. I typed in "flirty girl Lauren" and the screen asked, "did you mean Fleurty Girl?" Maybe I did.

Lauren Thom was a cute-as-heck fiery-haired twenty-nine-year-old single mother of three. Less than a year ago, she'd turned her $2,000 tax return into 300 printed t-shirts and sold them within a month. Now she had a successful online business and a store not far from On The Other Hand. The shop was in the front of the house and the whole family shared two rooms in the back. I wondered if it was wise for the NFL to be picking on adorable single mother entrepreneurs.

My spine tingled when I heard the chandelier crystals jostling down the hall. I waited to see if it would happen again. Then I went back to searching the web. I visited the shop's site and perused some of the local-centric shirts like "Brad Pitt for Mayor" and "There's no place like Houma."

The crystals clinked against each other again. I got up and made my way down the hall, hitting the light-switch on my way down. I opened the door to the big, empty bedroom I'd been warming up with a space heater and flicked the light-switch. The entire chandelier was swaying. I didn't remember a truck going by but I was too tired to make much more of it.

I went back down the hall, closed my laptop and turned off the tree then headed back into the bedroom to grab my nightie. The chandelier was hanging perfectly straight.

Chapter 15

Lillibette had heard about the "Brothels, Bordellos and Ladies of the Night" tour from her friend who went with a bunch of bridesmaids. We resisted eating beignets and wandered around the back of Cafe du Monde hoping to find a group gathered. A few tourists were laughing with a sassy woman in a red corset and fishnets, a rainbow tiered-tulle bustle and black combat boots. A wreath of tropical silk flowers encircled her blonde waves. Except for the tourism license hanging in her cleavage, she looked like Bette Midler in the "Divine Miss M." years. I leaned over to Lillibette. "I love her."

She smiled and we joined the group. "Miss M." called the smokers and other outliers close and introduced herself as Christine Miller. Ha! She really was the Divine Miss M. We walked through the Quarter learning about the underworld and tried to picture a street of restaurants and shops as a hotbed of gambling and criminal activity. The murderous prostitutes, Mary Jane "Bricktop" Jackson and Bridget Fury, sounded like a story ripe for a movie.

Some of the most interesting stuff was about the tradition of plaçage. Many of the European men had two families, a traditional one uptown and a common-law marriage contract with a free woman of color downtown. The men were often more playful with the children of these marriages and were bound to educate them. Because free people of color were allowed to own property in New Orleans, the common-law wives often owned beautiful homes. Our Miss M. talked about the Octoroon balls where women who were 1/8 black would be introduced to men of society in hopes of establishing a plaçage arrangement.

Miss M. made the Storyville district sound like a fun place. The neighborhood enjoyed a "decriminalization zone" for prostitution, like Vegas tucked inside the Quarter. The brothels were in beautiful homes and attracted some of the city's most distinguished men and their guests. We stopped for cocktails at May Baily's Place, a dark, cozy bar decorated with memorabilia from Storyville's days-gone-by when the bar was a brothel.

One wall was covered with copies of pages from the infamous "Blue Book." For some reason, the pages were all red. Like the *Blue Book* we use to value cars, the Storyville Blue Books listed madams, their assets (both personal and property) as well as "prominent" prostitutes. I read about the young and fashionable Miss Gertrude Dix "who was noted for keeping one of the best equipped places of its kind in this section of the States." Her attributes included her "palatial" home and the orchestra in her ballroom with "talented singers and dancers." I took a few photos in the low light.

Lillibette grabbed my arm. "Did you see these? It's the photos she was talking about."

Miss M. reminded us, "E.J. Bellocq."

The sepia photos were mesmerizing - feminine, fun and inviting. I recognized the one on the right immediately. I'd seen it many times but I couldn't have said where. The woman was sitting in a wooden chair resting her head on her hand and her arm on a table. Portraits of women and children hung on the lightly striped wallpaper behind her. Her crossed legs were boldly striped lengthwise in black and white. It reminded me of the circus but it was somehow perfect - like she was a kick to be around. Her "dress" looked like it might be a white shawl with long fringe or maybe a fancy tablecloth. It was tied casually over one shoulder. Her muffin-top hairdo tilted as she regarded the shot of rye in her hand with a bemused smile. It had the same mischief and quiet grandeur as the Mona Lisa.

I loved the way she was choosing to sell herself - as a good time, someone fun to talk to and easy to be with. I hadn't seen the other two portraits before. The one in the middle was an hourglass of a woman in thigh-highs and a simple tank top "dress" with a little lace on the straps. She was standing in front of a wooden door with her arms behind her back and her chin tilted up. She looked like a simple woman, slightly defiant - a plain-speaker. I noticed a thread hanging from the hem and wanted to burn it off.

The woman on the left looked like someone's sister, a teacher or a librarian. The portraits on the elaborately floral walls behind her were mostly of women and probably by the same photographer. A mirror framed by beautifully fashioned silver sat atop a gorgeous rich, wooden bureau. The relaxed woman gave the camera a sideways glance from her chair, her bare shoulders rounded over her lacy baby doll lingerie. A cigarette dangled from the fingers resting on her black-lace-stocking knee.

They all looked so serene and confident and interesting, not at all vacant and pitiful. I wanted to meet them and hear about their world and how they saw it. I liked that men of that era found them sexy without all the cartoon-perfection in pictures selling women now.

I was still staring at the women when Lillibette called me from across the room to see Miss May Baily's original license for the address to operate as a brothel. In a lit glass case below the license were some items from the bar's time as a brothel - a fan, a deck of playing cards, a silver flask and a watch. I guessed that husband had some explaining to do when he got home with a bare wrist. The fan was age-yellowed cotton lace. The flask was intricately carved with vines. There was a stamp or symbol of some kind pressed into the bottom. I stooped down to try to see it but the the stamp was hiding in shadows.

Miss M. came over to give us a five minute warning. Though she was only carrying a tiny red sequin purse, I took a shot. "Do you have a flashlight or somethin'?" Lillibette grabbed her chance at getting one last refill.

"Here." Miss M. twisted the "jewel" on one of her oversized plastic rings and it lit up. She took it off and handed it to me. "Are you trying to read something?"

"There's somethin' on this flask I'm trying to see. There." I pointed and tried to hold the ring-light steady while she leaned in. "What is that?" I stared at the symbol. I could have sworn it was the same symbol as the one on the chandelier.

Miss M. straightened. "Sometimes a plantation would have a stamp. It could be like a trademark for their goods or assets. Like a brand."

"But what is it? What is it a symbol of?"

She leaned back in. "A grasshopper? Is it an instrument? I'm not sure."

It was worth a try, "Is there some way to find out?"

Miss M. looked doubtful. "I can't imagine anyone knows anymore. They found this stuff during a renovation. And it's not like the men left a lot of clues as to their identities. I wish they'd found some of the women's clothes. Especially the stockings."

I motioned to her red fishnets. "Yours are cute."

She smiled, "Mine are just cheap fishnets. Theirs were like art. Like fashion or an Erté costume."

Lillibette joined me as I followed Miss M. out and we finished the tour in front of the house where Bellocq lived and took all those photos. It was the brothel and residence of "The Last Madam," Norma Wallace, a home-away-from-home for gangsters, politicians and movie stars - and those were just Wallace's lovers and husbands. She married her fifth and last husband at sixty-four, a twenty-five year old neighbor. After over forty years running a brothel, she was given the key to the city. It was hard to imagine anyone ever giving Heidi Fleiss the key to their city.

Afterward, Lillibette wanted to get a drink but I was excited to get home and work on my blog so she called a friend to meet her and I took the streetcar home. I was still getting my jacket off when my phone rang. Sofia.

"Hey. I just got back from this tour about prostitutes. It was pretty cool. I kinda can't stop thinking about it."

"Thinking about a career change?"

I laughed. "No, I thought I saw somethin' on a flask in an old brothel. It was a symbol but what's weird is I think I saw the same symbol on Sassy's chandelier. But, what's really weird is when I saw it on the chandelier, I thought I'd seen it somewhere else but I've never seen to that flask before. Never even set foot in that place before."

"Really? What's it a symbol of?"

Though she couldn't see me, I shook my head. "I have no idea. It's long and thin with other less-long things coming out of it. The tour guide thought it might be a grasshopper. Or an instrument."

Sofia chuckled. "So you really have no idea."

"Nope. She was cool though, you would've liked her. I'm putting a picture of her on the blog so you can see. She was dressed in a costume-version of the women from the brothels. You know, like corset and fishnets." I started thinking. Miss M.'s fishnets were cheap versions of the tights. Her clothes were made of cheap versions of satin and chiffon. I blurted, "What if the twins' other mother was a prostitute? What if that's why she didn't want to raise the girls? Maybe she didn't even know who the father was. Maybe it was just an occupational hazard in her mind."

"What?"

"The twins. Sassy's twins. What if their other

mother was a hooker? Then she might have clothes that were cheap versions of taffeta and chiffon, right?"

"Yeah, but you said she'd never chance the twins running into her. Wouldn't there be a chance they'd run into someone who worked in New Orleans? I mean, didn't they meet in the local laundry?"

I thought about that. "Yeah. Unless she got put in jail or killed or somethin' where Sassy knew they'd never see her around town."

Sofia sounded doubtful. "Yeah, maybe. So, wait. The flask at the brothel had the same symbol as whose chandelier?"

"Sassy, the mom of the twins. The woman who helped raise my mom."

"Right. So why would she have a chandelier with the same symbol as a flask in a brothel? Maybe her dad used to---"

"No, the chandelier came here from Texas a few generations ago."

"Oh. Then I have no idea."

I laughed. "Maybe the flask belonged to a tourist from Texas who happened to own the plantation the chandelier came from. That's a crazy coincidence if some plantation owner came down from Texas and went to a brothel just down the street from where his slave went after she was freed. Well, not really, I guess. I mean, there weren't that many cities back then and New Orleans was a huge port town. Heck, that chandelier was probably originally purchased here even if it did end up in Texas."

Sofia laughed, "And then back in New Orleans again."

"In my room!" I gasped. "Wait, I have to tell you. The chandelier makes noises sometimes."

Sofia hated ghost stories. It would be funny if it didn't upset her so much. "What kind of noises?"

"Like someone ran their fingers through the crystals. Only sometimes it's only on one side or just at the top. Or sometimes the whole thing is rocking back and forth. It's weird. I tell myself that it's a passing truck shaking the house but I've been writing down the times when trucks and busses go by and the times I hear the clinking noises and they don't line up. Not even a little. Like, not even by accident."

"I'm never staying with you."

"Understood."

Chapter 16

Sassy's house was so empty. Sure, there were boxes and newspapers and paint cans but everything Sassy was gone. Except the big screen TV. Chiffon was in Baton Rouge and Paris was in a bar somewhere but Taffy still put out a pretty good spread for the game. She'd arranged some folding chairs and tray tables in front of the TV. A few neighbors were saying goodbyes, heading to their own parties and urging Taffy to join them. The elderly woman wearing a Colston jersey briefly held Taffy's hand as she passed through the door. "All y'all can come. Bring the food if you don't want it goin'a waste."

"Naw. Thanks, but I gotta stay here. Mama would want me to be right here watchin' this here TV. Y'all go on. You got guests waitin'."

"Well y'all come over if you get tired of watchin' the Saints kick some Viking ass all by yourselves."

Taffy yelled to them, "Who Dat!"

They yelled back and Taffy waved then closed the door against the chill and rubbed the arms on her Drew Brees jersey. She spun to us with a devilish grin, "Drinks?"

Lillibette pleaded. "Come on Charlotte. Have a cocktail. This is the furthest the team's ever been. Ever."

I caved. "I'll take a beer if you've got one."

Lillibette clapped and disappeared into the kitchen. "Taffy, where's the fridge?"

Taffy laughed. "UncaParis sold it. Did alright by us, too. There's a cooler on the back stairs." She turned to me and motioned for me to take a chair. "Have you been lookin'? You find anything?"

I sighed. "Look, Taffy, I don't really know what I'm doin'. You get that, right? Like, no idea."

Lillibette yelled from the back door. "You got cups? Oh wait. I see them. I'm rinsin' this ice, Taffy, so I can put it in your drink. That okay? Don't suppose there's a koozie for Charlotte. Never mind, I see paper towels."

Taffy turned the volume up with the remote. "It's startin'!" She yelled to the ceiling where the chandelier used to hang. "This is it Mama! We makin' history tonight! Saints goin' to the Super Bowl!" She pointed at me. "You watch. We goin'."

I smiled. "I believe you."

Lillibette yelled carrying two go-cups and a beer into the room, "I believe! Who Dat!"

"Who Dat!" Wait, that was my voice.

Taffy turned the TV up even more. "Listen y'all. It's so loud in there. They rockin' that Dome. Vikings ain't gonna be able to hear a damn thing. You watch. Twelfth man! Man, I wish we had tickets to the Dome."

I turned to my cousin. "Lillibette, how did you not hook that up? That's your thing is gettin' us into places."

Taffy laughed. "Yeah, you slippin'. Back in the day, you'da gotten us seats and a limo."

Lillibette handed me the can of Bud wrapped neatly in a folded paper towel. "Yeah, well I don't date that limo guy anymore and Jonathan got more than a little tired of my guy friends hangin' around years ago so that's that. No more limos. No more ball tickets. No more free weed. That's where Jonathan messed up. Shoulda kept that weed guy around."

Taffy jumped from her chair, knocking it over. "What the... What? They just ran that ball in. First drive of the game and Vikings just scored. Damn." She closed her eyes and took a deep breath. "I believe."

The first half was an edge-of-the-seat-nail-biter with fumbles and recoveries into the last minute. The score was tied at the break. We retreated to the kitchen and filled plates with Zapp's chips and white-bread sandwich triangles. Taffy regarded my black turtleneck and gold earrings. "You need some Who Dat gear. I mean, at least you're not in purple. Jinx us."

Lillibette laughed. "Remember when you wore that brown and azure outfit on Bourbon before game day? Ha, Taffy, she was the onliest person in the world wearing brown and azure. And we were playin' Dallas so she was 'bout two paint chips away from a Cowboy."

I hit her arm playfully. "Come on now. It was a turquoise scarf with a brown jacket. They were all in navy and white."

Lillibette laughed. "You say navy, I say blue. Turquoise, azure, whatever, is blue too. Yee haw!" She pretended to swirl a lasso over her head.

Taffy high-fived her. "Well, I'm Azure too and

I'm gonna be way beyond blue if these boys don't come back lookin' ready."

We took our chairs and waited for the commercials to end. Azure is blue. Azure Taffeta and Violet Chiffon. Azure and Violet. What if it was a uniform? Maybe the twins' other mother was some sort of athlete. Maybe she was just passing through. A tournament or something. But wait, she'd be an athlete traveling with twin babies? Probably not. What about the circus? The circus must come here sometimes. Maybe she wore an azure and violet uniform while riding the back of an elephant. But, there were still plenty of places she couldn't have traveled freely during those Jim Crow years. Still, I might be onto something. I'd have to think about it.

I looked at Taffy and Lillibette staring intently at the screen. I'd seen that look a lot in the past month. The city was overflowing with hope and optimism. I wanted so badly for the Saints to win. It wasn't going to fix what The Storm broke but it was so clear that something was getting better here. Something was moving forward. As long as the Saints made it to the Super Bowl, the city would feel it had somehow accomplished something. A new slogan was on t-shirts and in windows, "Finish Strong." People here were used to losing but they wanted to make it to the show, play with the big boys.

I couldn't really remember what Taffy was like before The Storm but four and a half years later, Lillibette was like a deflating helium balloon, hanging in midair and resting on counters rather than pressing to get past the ceiling. I loved seeing her happy like this, energized. She finally cared about something again. And it was this game.

As an actor, I had to expand my mind past myself and try to figure out why people do the things they do, what they hoped to achieve, what reality they chose to see. Enough years thinking about people that way and it becomes apparent that people often create the world they imagine. I had no idea how the world worked but I did know that every time scientists set out to prove prayer doesn't work on things like disease, they've ended up proving it works - people can even heal a total stranger with nothing more than a name and prayer.

It seemed to me that with all these people praying, they ought to be able to shift the universe to their will. What if I really did believe? In showbiz, it could be dangerous to believe in anything. There were so many moments when your dreams could come true and then... they don't. So many almost-wins. Eventually, I learned to limit how much I invested in any one dream coming true. I never bet all my chips on any gamble. But what would it hurt to let myself believe this team that had never gotten this far in over forty years would actually make it to the Super Bowl?

I decided then that if we choose our reality, I would choose to live in the reality where people were dancing in the streets. I wanted to see actual dancing in the streets. Everywhere, not just Bourbon Street. I closed my eyes and pictured the neighbors we'd met earlier dancing outside. I pictured people honking horns and chanting Who Dats. Then I let my guts get tugged and yanked from joy to pain and back again as the game back-and-forth-ed its way to overtime.

We all waited while the refs made a decision about Meachem's catch. Inside the stadium, chanting started. "Finish Strong! Finish Strong!" If this were a movie, the underdogs who'd been through hell and back and never lost their soul would win. As Lillibette fanned herself with a napkin and Taffy paced, I closed my eyes and tried to watch the movie where the Saints got to go to the Super Bowl and everyone danced in the streets.

When the kick cleared the goalposts, I was sorta stunned. Taffy stood frozen. Even Lillibette just sat there shaking her head back and forth. Then we all screamed. "We're going to the Super Bowl! We're going to the Super Bowl! Who Dat! We're going to the Super Bowl!"

I ran to the door and threw it open just as the house next door did. The neighbors yelled. "Who Dat!?!" We all yelled. People were pouring out of their houses, screaming, hugging and crying. It was so beautiful it hurt. Then the music started as people drove by getting Crunk and horns blared - both car horns and brass ones. We ran down toward the Quarter just as a bus slowly rolled by honking out the beats to "Here we come to get you" while two young men in puffy vests danced on the roof. What few cars there were moved slower than the people dancing past them, around them and through them. Everywhere, people were dancing and hugging and shouting.

Corner parties formed throughout the city. Whole blocks shut down and gathered around DJ's or bands. We walked past a guy with a pick-up truck fully tricked out as a bar in the back. His prices seemed reasonable. A hunched elderly woman in a sparkly black-and-gold get-up pushed a shopping cart past us with a boom box rigged on it and Who Dat decorations all over it.

Taffy stayed behind with her neighbors and we kept walking until we found a block shut down between two bars with a DJ set up on a plywood riser. Hundreds of people danced to *Back That Azz Up*. There was a clump of about a dozen guys in jerseys "backing up" with wildly wiggling hips. A few of them wore quarterback Drew Brees' jersey but there were also jerseys for Bush, Shockey, Thomas, Colston and many more. It was like watching the team huddle shaking their "azzes." It struck me that football fans usually focused on one or two players but this was not a team about stars, this was a team about contributions. When everyone did their job, no one could "beat dem Saints."

New Orleans was like that too. The city was too full of "stars" for anyone to really stand out alone. The best known and most beloved were just as likely to have a Grammy or a James Beard Award as they were to be a crooked politician or a woman who roller-skated through the Quarter with a duck while wearing a wedding gown. Ruthie the Duck Lady was known for bumming smokes, drinks, meals and even a place to sleep from the people of the Quarter, but she was a valued part of local culture. Christine Miller had made a joke about her on the tour and I looked her up when I got home. There was even a documentary about her.

A brass band walked up and the DJ relented the floor as they second-lined us around to *When the*

Saints Go Marching In and several rounds of "Who Dat sayin' they gonna beat dem Saints!?!" Even the police joined in. We danced and sang and celebrated until it started getting light out and Lillibette needed to make it back across the lake. She honked her horn at every street party we passed the whole way back to the Garden District house. Then she turned to me and took a sip from a styrofoam cup. "You know you can't leave, right? The Super Bowl is on the seventh. That's barely more than a week. Only a fool would miss this. And it'll be Mardi Gras. It's the sixteenth this year. Do you have any idea how hard it is to find a place this close to the parade route? Seriously, you cannot leave. You'll hate yourself."

I was so bone-tired I was vibrating. And I was so elated from living in a dream-come-true all night that I was nearly drunk on euphoria. My brain was not to be trusted. "I'll think about it. Thanks for an amazing night."

She smiled and started to pull away. "Who Dat, baby! We're going to the Super Bowl!"

"Who Dat!"

Chapter 17

I had less than a week left before I was set to return to L.A. and it was getting harder to think of leaving New Orleans. Marilyn was still talking about the dress-opportunity window closing. Her new topic was pilot season and how TV shows were always looking for movie actors. She was convinced this would be our year. I reminded her no one went to my movie and the critics hated it.

She chuckled. "No one saw the movie but they all saw the dress and they know you have a movie out. That's enough."

I tried another tactic. "You would honestly leave this city right before the Super Bowl? You would just pack up and go right before Mardi Gras rolls a few blocks away? Honestly, Marilyn, this is like once-in-a-lifetime stuff. It's bucket-list stuff. It's you-had-to-be-there stuff. And I kinda think I shouldn't miss it."

"So you would stay another week?"

"Fat Tuesday is the sixteenth so I'd probably leave after that."

Her voice got high. "That's three weeks! You want to miss three weeks of pilot season?"

"I don't know, Marilyn. There are some things that are worth more than money. And there are a lot of things that are worth more to me than auditioning for maybe getting money."

She sighed. "Pilot's are the big money for smaller names."

"I get it, I do. I'm just thinking about it."

"Okay. But use the part of your brain that knows that you need money to live."

I laughed. "Okay."

I'd been looking for bookstores since my sister-in-law said she had a dream about me being in a local bookshop and meeting someone there. I kinda hoped it'd be cute guy but that was just habit. The first bookstore I'd found on a neighborhood walk was Borders, obviously not small or local.

You can tell a lot about a town by the books they read. The film section was much smaller than in the bookstores in Los Angeles, but the music section was much larger. Cooking was the biggest-by-far section and had dozens of subdivisions: local cooking, restaurant cookbooks, books about restaurants, books about restaurateurs, books from television shows or their stars (complete with TV's playing their cooking shows), wine, international cooking, and on and on. I used to collect cookbooks so I ended up burning a couple hours in there.

This time I was headed to the Garden District Book Shop. It certainly sounded more like the small local store from my sister-in-law's dream. There was a tour group forming in the lobby of the neighborhood shopping center. Many in the group had wandered into the cozy bookshop and were milling the local author and local subjects displays. I tried to keep an eye out for a cute guy as I glanced through a coffee table book of Garden District homes. It was kind of weird and wonderful being able to see inside some of the houses I passed on my walks.

A gentle-faced employee pointed at one of the pages. "That one's just down the street."

"Yeah, on Prytania, right?"

He looked up at me over glasses. "Oh, you live here?"

I guess it was still pretty obvious I wasn't from here. "A few blocks away. Do you have any books on New Orleans costumes?"

"Mardi Gras? Sure." He started to lead me…

But I stopped him. "No, like, I don't know, like uniforms?"

He looked puzzled. "I'm not sure what you mean. Band uniforms? Hotel uniforms?"

I regrouped. "I'm doing this wrong. Can you think of a uniform that would be like a cheap version of azure taffeta and violet chiffon? Like maybe an athlete or performer of some sort? Maybe something that would have passed through town? In maybe the 50's or 60's? Is there anything like that?"

"That's pretty specific." He looked around the shop a bit then back at me. "You know who might know is Miss Kay over at On the Other Hand. She's seen just about every costume and uniform in this city. She might have some idea who used those colors or those fabrics."

"Ha! I met her. She's awesome. Her husband, too." I put the book down.

"Yeah, they're great. That's who I'd ask."

I thanked him then headed to the food store on Magazine Street. In addition to the ever-increasing Saints decorations and Who Dat Nation flags, there were also handmade additions on lawns and in windows. Signs read "Pigs are gonna fly," "Super Bowl Bound" or just "Hell," but drawn to look like ice. And Saints fever was spreading. The rest of the country seemed to be getting caught up in the whole underdog story. People as far away as Canada and France were rooting for the Black and Gold.

The food store was festooned in Saints gear despite the coming of Carnival. Though there were stacks of purple, green and gold Mardi Gras King Cakes in bakery boxes, most of the cakes, cupcakes and cookies were decorated in helmets and black-and-gold fleur de lis.

I never knew when or where I was going to see something uniquely New Orleans. In the beverage aisle, a girl behind a card table handed out entire beers. She had big plastic go-cups so you could bring one with you around the store or outside. I got past her and a man was set up at another table handing out plastic cups of wine.

The man with the dreads and milky eye was standing on the corner when I came out of the store. His name was Albert and we'd taken to hugging our greetings. He always had a smile and a blessing for me so I was glad to see him.

I was beginning to love a lot of these little routines. I had routines in L.A. but I hadn't really missed many of them yet. I would miss walking this neighborhood, hugging Albert, shopping at local stores. I already knew what Sofia's opinion would be. Maybe that was exactly why I called her.

She laid it out plain. "It's kind of a stupid question, though, right? Um, should I go back to L.A.

to run around to auditions for shows I never get on the off chance that this is the year that I get one? OR, should I have a guaranteed once-in-a-lifetime experience? Um, duh."

"Okay, okay. But, just for one second, really think about what we're saying. This really could be the year. If I got a pilot, that's tens of thousands of dollars. If it runs, that's hundreds of thousands. If it gets renewed and is a hit, it's potential millions of dollars. I'm $60,000 in debt. That's real. I'm a slave to my rent so it takes minor miracles to have money left over for debt. It's crushing me, sitting on me."

She chuckled. "Yeah, but you go through this all the time and then - a few commercials and you dig your way out again."

"Sofia, seriously. Years ago, I did a budget to figure out how much debt I could afford to carry at one time. The answer was $64,000. It costs almost two grand just to put a roof over my head. Every month. I'm going to hit $64,000 really soon. Like, really soon."

"Or you're going to get a commercial really soon. Or a pilot when you get back after Mardi Gras. L.A. will still be here. It's just a vacation. Haven't you ever just taken a vacation?"

I chuckled. "Yeah, but it was usually somehow work-related."

Sofia laughed mischievously. "You should just play hooky once in awhile."

I laughed too. "I just had a high school flashback."

"Yeah, but I was right then and I'm right now. Take a vacation. This is ridiculous. If you come back,

I'm not hanging out with you until after Mardi Gras ends. Until... when is it?"

It was etched in my brain. "February sixteenth."

"That long? Wow, it's already been a long time to go without hanging out. But, who cares? We can sit and talk and eat and listen to music and crochet or whatever when you get back. No one in their right mind ever missed even a stupid vacation somewhere awful just to crochet with their friend."

"What about to keep a roof over their head?" I did have a point.

"Whatever. You'll figure that out. You always do. New topic or I'm hanging up."

"Okay, okay. Um, do you think L.A. is oversexed?"

Sofia was quiet a moment. "What do you mean?"

"Would you say that every decision, every purchase and every social event is somehow driven by sex?"

"That's oversexed?"

I nodded to no one. "Yes."

"Oh, then yes. Next topic."

I laughed. "The chandelier has been—"

"Next topic." She was laughing pretty hard now.

"I'm going to meet with the woman from the consignment shop. The lady with the hat and the husband who was a singing Santa."

She was still laughing. "Right!. The singing Santa who gave you cookies in a dress shop."

"You'd love that place and you know it."

"Probably." She calmed a little.

"I'm going to ask if she can think of any kind of uniform or costume that was azure and violet. It'd be

116

nice if I could help the twins find their other mother before I leave."

"In three weeks."

"Yeah, probably. I don't know. I just wish I didn't have this crushing feeling that I'm giving up on something I worked really hard to get for a really long-ass time."

"Yeah, well if it feels as good to get a TV series as it did to produce a movie, you should never come back."

I chuckled. "Yeah. You're probably right."

"I'm right a lot. That's why you keep me around."

"That and your carbonara. I can taste it just thinking about it." I really could - eggs, creamy cheese and crispy bacon tossed with pasta and black pepper. Yum.

"You're like the only person in that whole city wishing for food from L.A. right now."

I laughed. "No, only your genuine Italian food taught to you by your mom who barely speaks English who learned to cook from her mom who learned it from hers, just like the people here. I'm telling you, you'd love it here."

"You love it there and that's what matters."

"Yeah, I do."

Chapter 18

Miss Kay sat behind her desk smoking. She was wearing a black and off-white St. John's knit suit with big brass buttons. Strands of pearls dripped between her lapels. A wide-brimmed black dress-hat obscured some of her face. I extended my hand and she half-stood.

"Hi, I'm Charlotte. I called earlier."

"Yes, of course. Have a seat." She motioned elegantly toward a dainty chair she'd set up across from her. "So, you're looking for a costume?"

This was getting harder to explain. "Can you think of a costume or a uniform, from maybe the late 50's or so, that was made from a cheap version of taffeta and chiffon in azure and violet?"

"What kind of uniform or costume?"

I felt like I was wasting her time but she seemed like the kind of woman with a little on her hands for unproductive conversations with strangers. "I really don't know. The only other thing I can even think of that could help is it might be something worn by someone just passing through town."

"So, not a local uniform? Oh dear. That really takes it around the block, now doesn't it. Hmmm. Passing through in the late 50's?" She tilted her hat back and looked toward the ceiling. For awhile.

I started to feel insecure. "It's not much to go on.

I know I'm asking a lot for you to actually know but can you think of anything?"

She looked at me.

I took a shot. "What's the first thing you thought of? When I first described the colors and fabrics and era, you looked like you had a thought and then went into your memory. What were you trying to remember?"

She laughed. "I was walking on Bourbon looking at the supper clubs."

"The supper clubs?"

She smiled. "When I was a girl, Bourbon was the spot at night. There were all these supper clubs and night clubs and burlesque clubs. Sophisticated. I never went inside, of course, but there were posters with photos of some of the acts. There were regulars like the Oyster Girl, the Champagne Lady, Blaze Starr, of course, but they did also have visiting acts. Dancers, singers, contortionists, that sort of fare. I don't remember the photos being color so I couldn't help you with that."

"So, the burlesque dancers and different performers wore cheap versions of taffeta and chiffon?" That made sense.

"Yes. Although some items were quite fine. You know who might know more is Rick Delaup. He knows gobs about burlesque, especially in that era. He might even know who wore the costume you're looking for."

A thrill ran through me. "Really?"

"It's certainly worth a try. He's a delightful man so you'll be in good company in any case."

I couldn't wait to look Rick-the-burlesque-expert

up when I got home. Turns out he'd made a few films - *Ruthie the Duck Girl* was his fourth. Maybe it was a sign that he would have the answers. It was at least a sign that he was a pretty interesting guy. And a filmmaker. Never a bad idea to meet a filmmaker.

There was a graphic of a ticket stub on the top of the page reading, "Admit one." Wait, what did that torn ticket stub say? The one in Sassy's photo album. The Cloud. No! The Dream. Right. The Dream. Maybe Sassy knew exactly who the woman was and went to see her perform.

The phone rang. Claudia. "Are you staying for the game?" I was in love with her voice.

"Why? Should I?"

She chuckled her deep, smoky chuckle. "I have an audition for you, first week of February. It's a good one. A TV show about New Orleans. Will you be here?"

I was supposed to leave in two days. "How about this. Can you send me the information and let me get back to you tomorrow about my schedule?"

"I'm doing it right now."

The email popped up on my screen. I remembered back-in-the-day when I'd have to drive all over L.A. in horrifying traffic to pick up scripts. I loved email. "Got it. I'll call you tomorrow."

I was still reading the script when Lillibette arrived to take me to Krewe du Vieux. The parade wasn't officially the beginning of Mardi Gras but it had certainly become the unofficial starting gun. It was freezing so I was almost grateful we got stuck in a bottleneck as the lead float rolled past us announcing, "Krewe du Vieux's Fired Up." We found a good spot to stand and I took photos of devils and flame-wigs and a whole group of flying-pig-costumed people wearing pink wigs or pigs ears and white feathered wings.

A bright, green glove waved at me. It was the buy-you-a-drink guy. "Hey! You're still here."

He walked up and Lillibette shot me a devilish smile. I looked away. "This is my cousin, Lillibette."

She shook his hand. "Hey. Friend of Charlotte's?"

He clapped his green gloves together. "Charlotte. Did you tell me and I forgot or—"

"No, we never… And you are?"

"Tom." He smiled.

"Tom." I smiled too.

A float with a hands-and-knees-bare-ass-first papier-mâché woman passed with streamer-flames shooting out of her vagina. I felt like the moment needed commenting. "That's somethin' you don't see everyday."

Tom laughed. "You oughta get out more."

Lillibette nudged me then looked to Tom. "You're from here?"

"Born and bred. You?"

She smiled. "Plaquemine."

An amazing funky brass band walked by playing a song I knew some of the words to from long ago as a child.

Tom turned to me. "And where do you stay?"

I was purposefully vague. He was warm and friendly and fairly handsome in an everyman way but I didn't know him from Adam. "I'm over in the Garden District, not far from Magazine."

"Really? There not that many rentals around

there. Which house?"

There was no way I was answering that.

"Wait, not the yellow one with the blue shutters." How could he possibly know that? "The one with the horse buried in the back?"

Lillibette showed my hand so quickly. "Yes!"

I was totally uncomfortable and asked what Lillibette should have. "Why would you guess that?"

"A guy on my kickball team has been livin' there since the family turned it into apartments."

Lillibette jumped the gun again. "That's our family home. That's me. I'm his landlord. Jason, right?"

Tom laughed. "Small world. So, have you seen the ghost?"

Normally I would have laughed him off but I was stunned into silence. Lillibette jumped in. "What ghost?"

Tom rubbed his gloves together and blew on them. "Jason said the house is haunted. Weird stuff. Even stuff movin' or bein' messed with. He said one of those ghost tour guys told him that the family rode all the way from Arkansas or Mississippi or somethin' and the horse died when they arrived so they buried it out back."

I joked. "And it's been hauntin' the house ever since."

Lillibette corrected Tom. "It was Texas."

He continued. "Supposedly, they brought a chandelier with them."

Wait, what? "No, the chandelier came with the family of the woman that raised my mother."

A papier-mâché Bobby Jindal bobbed back and

forth into the back of an unhappy pelican. It may have been porn, but I gave it a lot of points for creativity, especially with the film-friendly title, "Jindal Drops the Pelican's Briefs." I snapped a photo.

Tom took the float in and kept going. "Maybe two families brought chandeliers from Texas. Maybe it was all the rage back then. Who knows? The tour guy said there's a ghost who guards a family secret."

Now I did dismiss him. "Come on. This is tall tale, sell-tickets showbiz stuff."

"Maybe so. Oh look, there's Uncle Lionel."

I looked at the natty man with the Barney Fife body and the Mack Daddy taste in clothes. He was surrounded by women from twentyish to closer to his advanced years. They were clearly only passing through but they looked like they were having a blast. I realized how normal it was to see people enjoying the moment here. No one seemed concerned if there might be someone in the crowd that could help their career or whether they were missing some more important party behind a velvet rope somewhere across town. The only people using their phones were taking photos. Everyone was present. I liked that.

When Tom saw the fire tuck approaching to end the parade he extended his hand. "Charlotte, it was good runnin' into you."

"You too, Tom."

Lillibette extended her hand as well. "Yeah, you too, Tom. Don't be a stranger. You know where to find us."

"That I do." He waved a green glove and disappeared into the crowd.

I spun on Lillibette. "He knows where to find ME. Not us. Just me, alone in a house."

"With a ghost."

She was joking but I didn't know what to say so I said nothing. Lillibette teased me about Tom all the way back to the house. I didn't want to admit I was a little afraid but I was glad the chandelier was still when I walked in. My phone rang and I jumped. I unlocked the phone's screen and pushed the button just before Sofia got sent to voicemail. "Hey! I just got home from the craziest parade. The whole thing was like penises and vaginas and political jokes. Wait 'til you see the photos."

"Penis and vagina photos?"

"Made of papier-mâché. They're funny. You'll see. I ran into that guy. The guy who bought me a drink when I got that job."

Sofia sounded intrigued. "So are you going out with him?"

"We exchanged first names. That's about it. But get this, he knows the guy who lives downstairs and he said a ghost tour guy told that guy that this house is haunted."

"Why do you tell me these things?"

I laughed. "I'm sure the story just got messed up somewhere along the way, but he said the chandelier came down with my family."

"Right."

I backtracked. "No, the chandelier came down with Sassy's family. Sassy's grandmother hung it in the house in the Treme when she moved here after she was freed. The only reason it's here now is it can't sit on the floor and they didn't have anywhere to put it for now. I'm just safekeeping it. Oh, that's what he said, he said that the story was that there was a ghost here guarding a family secret."

Sofia didn't laugh. "Okay, I'm officially creeped out now."

"Yeah, well I'm going to sleep under that chandelier tonight and I'm doing fine. You know what's weird though?"

Now she laughed. "Um, everything you said?"

"Okay, yes, fine. No, what's weird is we do have this family story about a chandelier but it's from like pre-Civil War times. My great-great-great-great grandmother lived on some huge plantation somewhere north of here. I remember reading in my Maw Maw's family tree in this photo album my mom has that this woman ran away with the overseer and her father disowned her."

"Why, what's the overseer?"

"He's like the boss of the slaves, the one in the fields with them. That's why the dad disowned her, because he worked in the fields directly with the slaves."

Sofia sounded surprised. "Your family owned slaves?"

"Yeah, well, you don't get to pick your heritage. But I always thought that was cool. I mean I know that my five-times great-grandfather was this huge slave owner but I'm the descendant of the one who left all of that for love. It wasn't written down in the album but Maw Maw once said she'd hauled a chandelier with her to Texas when she and her little sister ran off with the overseer. Maw Maw said it was the only thing she wanted from that place. I thought it was kind of kooky but romantic somehow."

"Did you ever ask if it was the same chandelier?"

Why hadn't we? "No, because I always heard the story about Maw Maw and Aunt Ava finding Sassy at the bus stop. But then Taffy told me that Mama Heck was actually the one who raised my Maw Maw so they've been with us for a few generations. But I'm pretty sure Mama Heck was already here when Maw Maw was born. Mama Heck's mother moved here when she was freed so that's way before Maw Maw was born, right?"

"I have no idea." Of course she didn't.

"Oh, I found out who might be able to help me find the other mother. I sent him an email through his website so I'm hoping to hear from him tomorrow. And I got another audition. A good one."

She stated rather than asked, "So, you're staying."

I laughed gently. "I should at least stay for the game."

"And Mardi Gras. Just think about it Charlotte. If they win, it's going to be an amazing party, right?"

I had to correct her. "I don't think anybody expects them to win. Getting there is plenty."

"Yeah, but if they do…"

I had to admit, "Yes, it would probably be the most amazing Mardi Gras ever."

"Just think about it. I know how much you love thinking about things. Or you could just decide and quit doing this one-day-at-a-time thing so you can actually relax and enjoy it."

She had a point. "I'll think about it."

Sofia cracked up. "Yes, you will."

Chapter 19

Lillibette said she'd heard about another unofficial parade that looked like it might be fun. She said men would be dancing and wearing dresses to honor a guy named Buddy D. Tomorrow was the first of February. I still wasn't sure whether to stay or go but either way, I'd want to enjoy a parade.

I looked up Buddy D. who turned out to be Buddy Diliberto, a beloved sportscaster who'd passed before The Storm. He'd promised that if the Saints ever made it to the Super Bowl, he was going to wear a dress and dance through the streets. Former Saints quarterback Bobby Hebert, who took over Buddy D.'s sportscaster job, declared himself leader of the parade in absentia and invited men to join him.

We took the streetcar toward the Dome. A tall, goateed man sat across from us and adjusted his handmade golden crown reading, "Saint Buddy." He was wearing a maroon satin bridesmaid dress bedazzled with, "Who Dat" and a fleur de lis.

I smiled at him. "You headin' to the parade?"

"We made it to the Super Bowl! I wouldn't miss this."

Lillibette looked for something in her purse. "How many guys do you think will show up?"

"This might be the biggest celebration we get to have for the Super Bowl so I'm thinking a lot. A few hundred maybe. A lot of the guys at my office were going."

I just had to know. "What to you do for a living?"

He smiled at my interest. "Me? I work in forensics." I tried to picture this tall drink of whimsical as a forensics expert. It was a tough fit.

We made our way up Poydras and it seemed like a pretty good-sized crowd was forming outside the Dome. By the time we got there, it was clear that thousands of people had taken this opportunity to celebrate the man and this moment. A brass band played on the sidewalk as we found a spot to watch the start of the parade.

A few dozen men assembled in rows wearing gold tennis shoes, white tube socks with red and blue stripes at the top, powder-blue gym-coach shorts, red satin jackets, white tank tops and terrycloth headbands. Lillibette laughed, "They remind me of high school. Who are they?"

"The shirts and jackets say '610 Stompers.' What's that?"

She shook her head. "Never heard of 'em. Maybe they're a dance team like the Pussyfooters. You know, those Mardi Gras dance groups they have for grown people. I've never seen men before, though."

The woman next to us in a pink wig leaned in. "Ever. They better be good."

The crowd went wild as the familiar *Stand Up & Get Crunk* refrain pumped through the speakers and the men began pumping their fists into the air. The ominous voice chanted, "Here we come to get you" as the men threw themselves into macho dance moves, punching into the air and playfully wiggling their hips. By the time they did their spins, the crowd was going bananas and I was having another one of my ever-more-frequent happy-cries at the beauty of it all. Everyone was laughing and dancing and singing along. Having come from D.C., New York and L.A., it was still new to me to be surrounded by so much joy.

After the Stompers danced away, thousands and thousands of men paraded past in pigtails, afros, beehives and fancy church hats. Most of the men pulled together black-and-gold ensembles. They were ordinary men - electricians, dentists, husbands and fathers. Some carried purses. Others carried coolers. They wore tutus and wedding gowns, prom dresses and Saints jerseys with skirts. Many carried Who-Dat-decorated black-and-gold second line umbrellas with fringe and feathers. Others carried signs reading things like, "We made it" with photos of Buddy D., "Super Bowl Bound" and "Screw Dat NFL."

The men seemed to be having the time of their lives but I couldn't help but notice how much fun the women in the crowd were having watching this shameless display of affection and silliness. It was hard to know when to take photos and when to just enjoy the spectacle of men-in-drag dancing past cheering Saints fans. Though I didn't get to snap a shot of him, I was glad I wasn't looking at the world through my camera when Tom walked past and waved wearing a Marilyn Monroe wig and a black cocktail dress with big gold flowers.

"Charlotte!"

I waved back. "Who Dat!" And he was gone. But it was kind of cool knowing someone in the parade.

A party truck called the "Tailgator" rolled up carrying Bobby Hebert, coworkers and friends. Their stereo was playing *It's Carnival Time* and we sang along loud and proud about feelin' fine. It was like experiencing some sort of city-wide hug to be in the middle of so many people genuinely feeling fine.

The parade stopped momentarily and the drinking buddies, families, elderly people and college kids chanted along with the people on the truck, "Buddy! Buddy!" I didn't know the guy from Adam but I had a feeling Buddy D. would have loved it, the whole thing.

Afterward, Lillibette headed back across the lake and I plugged in the tree then downloaded photos onto my laptop. I was still after-glowing and looking forward to seeing what I'd caught when I went to my room to change out of my jeans and boots. I rounded the corner and something grabbed my eye and stopped me in my tracks. The chandelier was hanging still but a single crystal was sticking straight out sideways.

I didn't move closer at first, just took it in searching for an explanation. I finally decided the wire must've gotten stuck and walked toward the lighting fixture to fix the crystal. As I reached out for it, the crystal dropped and swung back and forth. I grabbed lounge pants from a stack in a milk crate and ran out.

I grabbed my phone as it displayed Sofia's name and began to ring. "Hey!"

"Hey. You sound out of breath."

"Yeah. You don't want to know."

Sofia's voice got soft. "Ghost stuff?"

"So the good news is that it seems to be isolated to just the chandelier, which doesn't really jive with the whole thing about the ghost livin' here forever and guarding a family secret. The bad news is that freakin' chandelier hangs over my bed."

"I just couldn't."

I chuckled. "I know. But you're the one that told me to stay so get onboard. Tell me that it's probably nothing and even if it was, it seems content to play with the chandelier."

"That hangs over your bed where you sleep. No way. I could never."

I laughed. "Okay fine, give me nightmares, but I'm definitely stayin' for the game."

Sofia gasped. "You are? Oh yay. I'm so happy for you. You should just decide to stay for Mardi Gras. You keep making this like those snow days we hated in school. You know, when they'd say your school was going to be an hour late so you'd just stay in and watch a cartoon or something before getting ready to go to school again. Then they'd say it was going to be two hours late, but you've already pretty much burned one of the hours and now you're back down to really only having time for a cartoon or a nap. Then, after all that, they finally tell you your school is closed for the day. Only now, two hours are already gone before you can go sledding or make snowmen or whatever. It's like cruelty. And you're doing it to yourself. No one's making you."

I thought about that. She was right. "But, every week I'm here is another week I'm missing my moment and not making money - and I seriously need money."

"You already worked once there in New Orleans. And you don't usually get much work in January. If you had been here, for all you know, you wouldn't have gotten that part. Maybe you're profiting and you don't even know it."

"I hear you. I do. I'm just trying to be smart."

"Why?"

It was a simple question but it left me disarmed. Then I remembered. "Sofia, do you ever wonder why my career has never really taken off?"

"I figured it was because you started old."

I laughed. "True dat. But there's this other thing I do where I come to these moments and choose the road less traveled instead of just doing what works. Remember the beauty pageant in South America? I could've stayed and been launched as a model and a member of society. I won everything from a modeling contract and a year-long membership at the country club to ballet lessons with a prima, dinner with the President and a round-trip ticket to Rio. And I left it all to finish two months of high school - and I only needed one class to graduate. I could've totally gotten my GED later and maybe been an international model."

"Isn't the only reason you modeled was to help pay for college?"

"Of course, I'm just sayin' I could've seized that opportunity and I walked away."

Sofia got insistent. "No, you walked toward. You always wanted to go to college. Heck, you kept on going and got a master's. Look, you just found a new way to make money. That's all the modeling thing was about. You never wanted that life."

"I know. I'm just sayin' it was put in front of me and I walked away. Maybe that's stupid. You know how many people would kill to have those kinds of opportunities? I don't want to be stupid or stubborn or narrow-minded or somethin'."

It sounded like she was chopping vegetables now. Nia was singing in the background and I could picture her spinning in one of her princess dresses. Sofia chopped and talked. "It's not narrow-minded to know that you don't want to be famous."

I sighed. "I really don't. I mean, I like getting treated like a famous person sometimes but I never wanted people to care about who I'm dating or dig through my trash or whatever. Like, I get it that the whole point of a career is to keep doing bigger and better things and I really do want to do bigger and better parts, but—"

She laughed. "Bigger and better than having a few lines in your underwear when you trained to do Shakespeare?"

"I'm over the whole I-studied-Shakespeare thing. But yeah, it'd be great to do bigger, better parts. But mainly, I just don't want to feel like I'm choosing to walk away from an opportunity again. Marilyn says this is my moment and I'm missing it."

Sofia laughed. "Okay, it's SO not the same thing as the beauty pageant. You had already won those prizes. And you came home with money and a fur coat and stuff. Actually, in this case, New Orleans is the place where you already know you'll win the prize of being there for this amazing party. And if they win—"

"I know, I know. I see what you're sayin'. But it's

not a great analogy since finishing school had a concrete outcome of me gettin' my diploma and goin' to college, so really staying here is like staying in South America but without all those prizes to help launch me."

"Whatever. You should stay. If they win - you stay. Promise."

"Fine, if pigs fly, I'll stay." I remembered. "Oh hey, I saw that guy again, Tom. He was walkin' by in the parade today and waved to me. Oh my gosh, Sofia, you would've loved this parade. I won't go into the whole thing. I'm going to blog about it but wait until you hear what he was wearing. He looked like Marilyn Monroe over the subway grate in a black-and-gold floral dress."

"Why?"

"You'll see. I'm going to write it and do the photos when we hang up. The guys are so different here. It's kinda messin' with me. They seem so much more happy, like for-real happy. And fun. I mean, the women do too, which is awesome, but I… I can't believe I'm sayin' this after the debacle that has been my dating life for the last few years, but I think I could date the guys here. They just don't seem to be in any hurry. I like that. And they really don't seem to care at all whether anyone thinks they're powerful or cool or whatever. It's relaxing."

"You're totally staying and you're going to ask that guy out when you see him again."

I laughed. "That's my point. You know I don't do that. If a guy isn't man enough to ask me out for a proper date, he's not man enough for me. Whatever, I'm just sayin' I'm the tiniest bit intrigued."

Sofia laughed. "Yeah, you're totally going to go out with that guy."

"I'm hangin' up. I have to do the photos and work up the courage to sleep in my room."

Sofia got quiet. "Seriously Charlotte, smudge the place or something."

But I had to admit, as much as it scared me to think I might not be alone in this house, there was something about the chandelier shenanigans that lit my imagination. I couldn't help but wonder what it was all about. If it was some sort of supernatural thing, why the chandelier? Did it mean anything? And if it was some sort of entity, who could it be? Was it one of my ancestors? Did I know them? I pushed it out of my head and set my photos to slideshow.

Chapter 20

I wasn't sure whether to be more excited about my second audition in New Orleans or about meeting with Rick Delaup, the burlesque expert, afterward. I hopped a streetcar downtown and ran my lines surrounded by tourists and the sensible-black-shoe-wearers headed to work at restaurants and hotels. One young woman bopped to headphone music and carried a giant laundry sack. I hoped it was a sign that I'd find answers today.

I didn't think I was right for the part, but I felt pretty confident that I'd impress the casting director. I was a highly-trained, seasoned pro, a big fish in a small pond. I would kill it.

The office wasn't glamourous. At all. I looked for the computer to scan my bar code... and found none. A sign-in sheet sat affixed to a clip board on the desk. The young assistant looked up a little from under her bangs. "Headshot?"

How many times had I told actors that headshots were like umbrellas - better to have one and not need it than to need one and not have it. But L.A. had converted to digital years ago so we'd all gotten in the habit of only bringing a headshot if it was requested. Now, it was raining and I had no umbrella. I felt like a rookie. I even felt a little embarrassed - something actors rarely have time for in an industry where we used to have to print our weight and sizes just to audition. The barcodes had all that information as well as the headshot. All I had now was a useless code and a cavalcade of lame apologies about being on a vacation and not having my work materials, yadda, yadda. After telling actors to always bring a headshot, I would always tell them to never apologize. I honestly couldn't believe how badly this was all going.

I sat and focused on my lines. I wasn't right for the part of "harried Parole Agent," but I was here to impress this casting director and Claudia, who I still hadn't met. Which was weird. I was so used to hoop-jumping before an agent would invest in me, and agents really loved meetings and signed-paperwork in my experience. Claudia was more like Charlie in *Charlie's Angels*, a whisky voice sending me on missions.

I really wanted to be a part of this show. *Treme* was the next offering from the geniuses behind *The Wire*, a 2002 series that was still considered to be the best show ever on television. *Treme* was set six months after The Storm and would include local characters and musicians playing themselves.

Once I was in the room, I was back in the groove. The casting director was intimidating - she was probably a wiz at poker. But I'd been at this long enough to know that didn't mean she wasn't impressed.

Afterward, I shook it all off and walked to the French Quarter for my meeting with Rick Delaup. I'd been walking these blocks since childhood but I didn't really know the order of the streets. It was one of those rare moments I wished my phone was connected to the internet. I stopped into Forever New Orleans, the store that used to be my balcony restaurant, and approached the sales clerks chatting behind the counter.

The one with a bow in her blue hair held her phone up to the one wearing an LSU turtleneck. "Look! They won!" She thrust the phone at me. "Did you see this? They won!" She pulled the phone back before I could read it.

LSU girl grabbed the phone and stared at it. "I can't believe it!"

I began to wonder if I'd somehow missed the Super Bowl. "Who won?"

The girl with the bow smiled. "Lauren and them. The NFL conceded that they don't own 'Who Dat.' They dropped the cease and desist. We never win. I can't believe we won."

I noticed she'd switched from "they won" to "we won." I'd worked in retail for ten years and had mastered the art of "ownership." At some point in the sales pitch, I'd switch from "That color brings out your eyes" type-talk to "When you get this home, you should try it with strappy heels." Bow-head girl was taking the shop owners' victory as a citywide victory, as her victory. Maybe pigs really would fly. If five local shops could beat the NFL, why couldn't the Saints beat the Colts? I was starting to believe it could happen. And it felt kind of exhilarating.

I got directions to Tujague's and left the elated, hugging girls to their celebration. I dug in my backpack when my phone vibrated against my spine accompanied by the comes-with-the-phone ringtone fighting to be heard over street musicians and laughter. As usual, I caught it just before it went to voicemail. Claudia. Really? Even for fast-paced TV production, I shouldn't have feedback yet. "What's up?"

"I have a meeting for you. It's a local director. He's putting a movie together and wants to talk to you about a role he'd like you for. He's a fan of your work."

"Really?"

"The money's still coming together but I've read the script and it's good. He's great. You'll love him."

"Cool. Call back and leave the details."

"Great. Hey, did you hear about the NFL?"

I chuckled. "Yes. Great news. Pretty amazing."

Claudia laughed her smoky laugh. "Pretty amazing? It's unicorns flying past pigs over a frozen hell."

I laughed. "Who Dat."

"Go Saints!"

I didn't like the sound of, "The money's still coming together," but in my experience, the smaller the budget, the bigger and better my part was.

Tujague's featured a beautiful bar with giant mirrors and tall wooden columns. I approached a fit man with wavy, brown hair and hoped it was Rick. He stood from his barstool and smiled. "Charlotte?"

"Oh good." I smiled and we shook hands.

"Did you hear about the NFL?"

I laughed. "Good news travels fast."

"It's baffling news. We never win anything. Especially when it comes to football. Wait. You're not from here. Are you a Saints fan?"

"Do I have a choice?" I ordered a Diet Coke and Rick got his coffee refreshed.

He stirred a dollop of cream into the rich roast. "So I have to ask. Where did you hear about the costume? You're certainly too young to have seen it yourself."

"Wait, you know what costume it is? Are you serious? What is it?" I knocked the straw in my glass almost toppling it.

He grabbed the base of my glass and smiled. "I'm pretty sure I know the costume. Did I just distract you too much to tell me where you heard about it?"

"Yes. No! No, of course not. You did all that work and I'm a total stranger. It's actually a great story."

He smiled. "My favorite kind." So I told him about Sassy and the laundry basket and the woman saying "You want 'em?" I told him about the will reading and the names having meaning. He loved the names, "They're perfect for burlesque dancers."

I laughed.

"Thank you. A great story, as promised. So, I don't know the name of the dancer but I remember seeing a poster from Madame Francine's on Bourbon. Fat Catz is there now. Have you been there?"

I smiled wide. "Yeah, actually, I have. So it wasn't anything to do with 'The Dream?'"

"It's curious. Where did you get that?"

"It was Sassy's. It was on a ticket stub that had been torn in half."

He slapped his hands together like he was swiping cymbals. "Ha! One door down from Madame Francine's was a dance hall called 'The Dream Room.' I thought I remembered them being segregated but Fats Domino played there so maybe they had exceptions or I've misremembered."

"Tell me about the costume. No, tell me about who wore it."

"I'm not really certain who the dancer was but I remember the costume because it was a mermaid and I remember wondering if she did a water act. It was a purple taffeta bustier with these turquoise ruffles on the hips pointing upward like fins or something." He illustrated with his hands, running them over his hips and outward. "No shell-bra or seahorse earrings, just strands of pearls across her arms like straps that had fallen. The hips to the knees was aqua sequin." He flicked his hands outward at his knees. "And then turquoise chiffon came down shorter in the front, almost exposing the knees, and longer in the back. Really flowy like water. It was pretty elegant in a cheesy sort of way."

"Wow. It clearly left an impression. Where did you see the poster?"

He smiled big. "That's the good news. The poster is probably long gone but the son who grew up in that club is still around and he might remember a mermaid. I can put you in touch with him." He picked up a napkin and grabbed the bartender's pen from a cup below the bar. "What's your number? I'll track him down and see if he's taking visitors."

I felt that familiar dread of a stranger asking for my number then remembered that, so far, zero men had actually hit on me in New Orleans. I took the pen and wrote my number. There was something comforting about him not just using technology and entering it in his phone. It's what I would've done.

"So you'll call him and let me know? Does he usually take visitors?"

"It's not usually Mardi Gras and it's never the Saints in the Super Bowl."

I laughed. "Right. Of course."

"I can't believe the NFL gave in. What a kick in the pants."

"As *Scarface*'s Tony Montana said, 'Every dog has his day.'"

He laughed. "Amen."

Chapter 21

The game was in Miami but everyone knew the party would be here. Lillibette thought it would be best if we started Super Bowl Sunday in the French Quarter. "If they don't win, I'd just as soon not be in the Quarter, but I'd hate to miss bein' there before the game while we're still winners."

That made a lot of sense to me. This wash of optimism and pride was just hours away from potentially bursting and being replaced with a "We'll get 'em next year" vibe more familiar to everyone.

We had to walk since the streetcars were all down for the Mardi Gras parades and the buses were showing up whenever nowadays. It was hard to believe two such giant moments were happening at the same time. It's tough to grasp how big and varied a party Mardi Gras is if you've never been. And it was hard to process all the feelings I had seeing the Dome in the distance. That icon had been like a logo for the failures, losses and horror of The Storm. I couldn't help but happy-cry thinking of how gleaming and full of promise it looked now.

The tail-end of the Krewe of King Arthur parade rolled down St. Charles in front of us. We caught up to the floats and bands at Canal Street and joined the throngs of people reaching for beads, toys and doubloons. I ended up with so many beads that I started getting a neck ache as we made our way down super-packed Bourbon Street. We stopped several times to dance with a brass band as balcony dwellers threw beads down to the crowd.

I followed Lillibette into Fat Catz. She brushed her thick, blonde bob off her shoulder and yelled to me over the crowd and the music. "In case this was good luck for 'em. Remember? We came here before the Vikings game."

I pulled her back outside where she could still barely hear me over the chanting of Who Dats. "I forgot to tell you! I might've found Taffy and Chiffon's other mother."

"Who is she?"

"I don't know yet, but this burlesque expert thinks she may have danced here back when this place was a place called 'Madame somethin'.' Francine maybe. I have it written down. Anyway, two doors down used to be a dancing hall that I think Sassy had a ticket stub for. There's a chance she saw the poster for the woman. Maybe she even went in and saw her dance. Heck, maybe Sassy knew exactly who she was when she saw the mermaid costume in the laundry. That's what the burlesque guy thinks, that the fabric in the laundry basket was a mermaid costume of a woman who danced here for a little while. Maybe that's why Sassy decided to keep the girls. Maybe she understood the life they were in for the minute she saw that fabric she'd seen on the poster. Maybe that's why she said, 'I did all I could to give y'all a name that meant something.' It was the other mother's identity - the mermaid dancer, and it was the reason the twins were better off with Sassy. If

I were playing her, that's what I would've used to make this all make sense."

People started dancing and chanting next to us. Lillibette shouted. "Are you going to tell Taffy?"

"Not yet. The burlesque guy is tryin' to put me in touch with a guy who grew up there. Here. In Fat Catz, back when it was Madame whatever. He might know her name or have the poster or somethin'. I'm gonna wait to see if I get anything from him before I tell the twins."

We let ourselves be pushed inside toward the dance floor and joined the pre-game festivities. But as the crowd became drunker and rowdier, I was glad we'd decided to spend the game Uptown among neighborhood locals. We left Fat Catz early enough to make it back but hadn't counted on the non-stop party gauntlet that Bourbon Street had become. In keeping with the Super Bowl/Mardi Gras theme, many people wore black-and-gold jester caps. I spotted a Jesus with long hair and a robe emblazoned with "Breesus Christ" and the number nine. He held a Mardi-Gras-beaded staff with a golden football on top.

Things got super-quiet when we finally exited the center of town then church bells clanged, marking fifteen minutes until kickoff. And they kept clanging in the distance behind us as we made our way up Magazine Street to a local haunt with pool tables and a black-and-gold-wearing crowd. I still hadn't bought any Saints gear so my turtleneck and the gold scarf Lillibette leant me would have to carry the day.

I had a little riding on the game. I'd promised Sofia that I would leave it to the Saints - if they won,

I'd stay through Mardi Gras. But the city had a LOT riding on this game. Win or lose, they'd party afterward. Win or lose, rain or shine, the Saints parade was schedule to roll between regularly scheduled parades. But I knew that a win would mean more than I could even fathom to a people who'd been through so much loss.

The game was another nail-biter, but I'll be honest - it didn't look good for the Saints at halftime. I thought about all the statewide prayer that went into this day. I thought about the priests who wore their jerseys over their robes and led second lines in their churches. I thought about the exotic dancers standing seductively in the doorways of Bourbon Street wearing Saints bikinis. I thought about the elegant elderly women arguing over the defense strategy, the children running around in jerseys playing football between parades, the stores and houses festooned in Who Dat Nation regalia.

Didn't every dog have his day as Tony Montana insisted? I had been considered ugly and dressed "wrong" in high school then went on to make money for college as a model wearing the very finest and fashionable of clothes. Heck, the same people who called me ugly in school now paid to watch me in movies. Maybe the quarterback no one wanted and our merry band of misfits really could win the Super Bowl. I'd seen far stranger success stories in L.A. Heck, the Terminator was my governor. Pigs flew and hell froze over all the time in Hollywood.

So, when the second half opened with a recovered onside kick and a touchdown, I started believing in flying pigs and wanted to stay and see what the biggest and best Mardi Gras ever would look like. Then as the last seconds of the game wound down and we were fourteen points ahead, it began to dawn on everyone that we were about to win the Super Bowl. For real. And then, with the entire Who Dat Nation holding their collective breath - the game ended and the bar exploded with cheers. There was no crying this time. It was a straight-up celebration right away that immediately spilled onto Magazine Street.

We got Crunk and hugged strangers and Who-Datted our brains out. The Garden District security patrol and half-a-dozen NOPD cars rolled by honking their horns, sounding their sirens and yelling Who Dats out their windows at the drinking, dancing, hugging crowds. Some even waved kerchiefs like they were in a second line parade.

A kid ran by in a Brees jersey waving a Who Dat Nation flag. His little sister ran behind him wearing a helmet and a Saints cheerleader outfit. A fire engine passed slapping high-fives and letting revelers with go-cups hitch rides on the back platform. A cab driver stopped near us and yelled, "I am loving this very much" with a thick foreign accent. He held his hand up and a beer-toting college kid ran out to slap it and exchange Who Dats. An elderly woman danced past, limping on one leg with her walker held high in the air. A guy stopped in front of us and yelled, "Hell freezes!" then ran off while some people just plain screamed at each other. "AAAAAAAAH!"

Joy flooded the streets. Laughter, high-fives and pride flooded the streets. Music and spirit and soul flooded the streets. Love and joy flooded the streets.

The whole city flooded with victory. Then, Queen's *We Are the Champions* emanated from inside the bar and everyone inside and out sang at the top of their lungs. As Freddie Mercury led them to the lyric they could barely bring themselves to believe, I saw it dawn on all their faces - that we were the champions... OF THE WORLD!

We danced the Cupid Shuffle then a band walked up playing *When the Saints Go Marching In* and we all started singing along. A trumpeter pushed through and joined in as people spilled out on balconies and sang about wanting to be in that number when the Saints marched in. And we were in that number. I was in that number when the Saints went marching in. We screamed loud and proud after the chorus, "Who Dat! Who Dat! Who Dat sayin' they gonna beat them Saints!?!" We chanted it three times like always but this time was different. Then someone yelled, "We Dat!" Exactly.

Lillibette and I danced and sang and watched young guys trying to outdo each other with flips and cartwheels. We hugged and Who-Datted for hours. But I noticed something funny. All night, people came up to me with the same dazed face, the same question, "Can you believe it?"

After months of hanging "I Believe" and "Believe Dat" posters in windows and on doors, no one could make themselves believe it happened. Pigs flew, hell froze over and it really, really happened. The Saints won the Super Bowl. Who Dat!

Chapter 22

It was hard to believe anyone was trying to get anything normal done. Sure it was a Monday with no parades but no one had slept, everyone was hoarse and most were seriously hungover. I wasn't much of a drinker but my voice was shot and so were my eyes. It wasn't how I pictured this meeting with a local director going. He said he didn't have the money for the movie yet but he had a good track record for getting his projects made and distributed. Claudia had vouched for him so I let myself be flattered that he wanted me for one of the leads, though I was used to these things falling through. I reminded myself that anything could happen - the Saints had won the Super Bowl.

We sat in the window of a local coffee shop discussing the script's themes and the two lead female roles. I jumped when someone tapped from outside. The burlesque tour guide waved at me from the sidewalk. She was wearing a metallic gold wig with a Who-Datified tiny top hat and a black faux fur coat. We waved back and she went on her way.

The director sipped his coffee. "Friend of yours?"

"She does a tour on brothels and bordellos. My cousin and I went."

"You went to brothels?"

"It was more like a historical tour, but yeah, we

saw a couple places that used to be brothels and one of them is a bar now so we went in. They had photos of some of the Storyville women and these like menus of services but they weren't sexual per se. It was more like, this lady is known for her well-appointed parlor equipped with a string quartet or whatever. It was all pretty cool. And she was a great guide. You should go. It was fun."

He smiled wide. "Sounds like you're really enjoying the city."

I smiled too. "Yeah. I've been coming here all my life but it was always for short bursts. Sometimes just driving in from across the lake to go dancing on Bourbon. This is the longest I've been here. And, it's just really… it's been kinda magical."

"How long have you been here?"

I thought for a moment. "Like, two months?"

"That's long enough. I've met people who've only come for a weekend and just… never left."

I warmed my hands on my cup of tea. "Yeah, well they probably didn't spend the last couple of decades studying and scrapping their way in the one percent of this industry that makes enough money to live. And it's the entertainment industry - the one everyone wants to be in."

He looked out the window at Albert passing by. I waved to Albert and he waved back. I looked to the director. "He's a friend. First friend I made here without my cousins having anything to do with it."

"Well, I hope you just never leave. I can be your second friend you met without your cousins."

I chuckled. "You might have to wait in line behind Claudia. She's awesome. But she's my agent really and I'm not sure how deep a friendship can run when you've never met the person."

He laughed big. "Yeah. Good luck with that."

I was kind of startled. "Really? Why?"

His eyes got big. "You're in good company. I know a lot of people who owe her a lot who've never met her."

It was actually hard to process. I lived in a world where people battled to be seen and known. They fought to get on red carpets and talk shows, magazine covers and billboards. It was hard to imagine someone becoming the most powerful agent in town without shaking a lot of hands and buying a lot of lunches. "You're kidding. Seriously?"

"You'll see."

We walked out to his no-big-deal car parked in front of a tobacco store. In L.A., his move would have been to say goodbye to me then get on his phone until I was out of sight before going anywhere near this regular-old-blue-four-door-from-Japan. I really did love how relaxed people were here. They seemed confident they were enough. I hadn't seen one Prada bag or McLaren since I got here. It was hard to even imagine anyone trying to drive one of those half-million dollar cars over these pothole-riddled streets.

The director wished me a happy Carnival then hugged me goodbye. Over his shoulder, I spotted a logo on the glass door of the tobacco shop. It was an old-fashioned pipe curved like a tiny saxophone the same way my dad's was when I was a little girl. It'd been so long since he quit, I'd nearly forgotten about his constant puffing and the sweet smell of cherry tobacco drifting inside the car before he'd crack the window. I used to love that pipe. It was pretty - smoothly polished laurel-root wood with some small carvings on the bowl. But I loved it because when it was around, it meant Dad was around.

It wasn't until I got home and checked in to see what the chandelier was up to that I remembered one of the carvings. On the back of Dad's pipe, where the bowl met the shaft, was a tiny carving of the same symbol I'd seen on the bottom of the flask at Miss May Baily's. That's why it was so familiar.

I had to call Sofia and get her up to speed. She sounded surprised. "Wait, you're not calling to say how the meeting went? Okay, I'll drop it."

"No, it was great. He was great. He even said he'd be my friend if I were here. And I believe him, which is the really weird thing. But, no, you're missing the point. If the symbol is the same one that was on the flask, it's also the same one on the chandelier. That's what made me think of it."

She clanged plates she was washing. "Okay." I could hear Nia laughing at the TV.

"That chandelier was Sassy's. Sassy worked for my mom's family, not my dad's. Why would she have the same symbol on her chandelier as he had on his pipe?"

"And the flask. So maybe it's like a brand name or something and it's on lots of things."

"A pipe, a flask and a chandelier? That's more variety that Wal-Mart sells. These things are from like the 1800's. And they're from different locations."

She turned the water off. "That's weird."

"Right?" I was glad I had a witness to the

weirdness.

"Wait, but what was the symbol again?"

"I don't know. An insect? A weapon? An instrument?"

She laughed. "Well, that's no help."

I laughed too.

"What did you think it was when you were a kid?"

I tried to remember. "I guess I thought it was a bird's head and neck, like a crane or something with crown feathers but my brother said it looked like someone standing and peeing."

Sofia was really laughing now. "I have to see this symbol. It's like that blotter test where everyones gets something different and it reveals how you see the world."

"Rorshach."

It took her awhile to stop laughing long enough to clarify. "Horse shit?"

"No! Rorshach."

She was cry-laughing. "Horshack?"

Now I was getting punch drunk with laughter too. "No, Rorshach. The blotter test. It's called the Rorshach test."

"Oh, I thought maybe you were talking about that guy on *Welcome Back, Kotter* and I couldn't figure out what that had to do with your worldview."

"And horse shit came to you first? Damn, I must really sound like a cynic."

She started to calm. "Not lately. But seriously, it's probably a symbol for something common back then and it's just on a lot of stuff."

"Probably. But that guide said it could be for a

plantation, like marking their name on their things. Oh, I saw her today. She walked past the window while I was at my meeting. She stopped and waved at me through the window."

"That's friendly."

I laughed. "It's a friendly town. I used to say that here there are no strangers - only friends you hadn't met yet."

"Nice."

"Yeah."

We hung up and I snuggled into bed. I stared at the chandelier above me glinting in light from a nearby streetlamp. I wished I could see the symbol on the fixture one more time just to make sure I hadn't made it all up. It had to stand for something recognizable, didn't it? And how did it end up on my dad's pipe, a chandelier in Sassy's family and a flask in a Storyville brothel? It just seemed like more than coincidence for such a uniquely indecipherable symbol. What the hell was that thing?

Chapter 23

Some people were calling it Lombardi Gras, some called it Dat Tuesday. The Victory Parade was expected to attract at least 200,000 people - which was extraordinary when you considered the city's population was about 385,000. Lillibette called from the interstate and said the traffic was unprecedented and she'd just meet me there on the corner of St. Charles and Canal.

It was bitter cold with an icy wind and there was a threat of rain. As I walked toward town, it seemed as if the entire city were answering a clarion call. Families spilled out of their houses pulling wagons full of children, coolers packed with beer and the occasional ladder-with-a-seat-on-top-with-wheels-for-dragging. People were parked on sidewalks and in medians - known as neutral grounds here.

I met a nice man who worked at the Double Tree hotel and we walked halfway together. His father had passed but had always dreamed of this day. The guy was hoping to catch some beads to put on his father's resting place.

I was about three hours early for the start of the parade but it was already packed by the time I hit Canal. Lillibette texted that she was still stuck so I wandered a little before finding a spot. I made some more insta-friends, people from Hammond,

Napoleonville, even Alabama and Mississipi. Everyone said the same thing, "I couldn't be this close and miss it." I texted Sofia, "You were right. Glad Im here."

There were twelve floats scheduled, a fairly short parade. And it was only going a few miles, not the regular seven-to-eleven mile Mardi Gras parade stretch. All the floats had been donated by various Mardi Gras krewes so I was expecting a hodgepodge of themes. The crowd only had one - Saints fans.

Lillibette tried to call but it dropped. She texted, "Just parked. Walking."

I texted back, "SW corner."

I had to think about her next text. "Uptown or DT?"

I pictured the city. "Uptown."

"River or lake side?"

"River." I wasn't sure what all the clarification was about but I figured it was one of those things like, "Where did you go to school?" where everyone here knew they meant high school, though the rest of the country agreed that meant college.

It seemed like I waited a long time for Lillibette. I began to wonder if I should be worried. I looked around to see if I could spot her in the sea of black-and-gold-clad fans. I'd never been so glad her hair was such a honey-white blonde. I found her head looking around on the northwest corner.

I tried calling but the phone wasn't working. I tried texting but the network was shut down due to overuse. I remembered Lillibette saying the same thing happened during the Super Bowl. One by one, the networks went down. I pushed closer to the barricade to see where I could cross the street. But there were no breaks in the barriers. And no kids playing in the street. In fact, only the police were in the street. I yelled to one and he smiled and walked over. "You okay?"

"Yeah, I see my cousin over there and wondered where I should go to cross."

"Sorry, no crossing today. Where you are is where you are."

I smiled. "They're not going to be here for at least another hour. I can't just cross? My cousin's right over there. I can see her."

He chuckled. "Yeah, not going to happen today. Grow where you're planted. Geaux Saints! Who Dat!" And he was gone.

I tried shouting Lillibette's name but it was drowned out by voices on top of voices like a thick cloud of sound. The college-age kid next to me looked across the street to see who I was yelling for. "You lost someone?"

"My cousin's over there. I can see her but my phone's down."

His friends chimed in. "Mine too." "Yeah, mine too."

He gathered his group of about a dozen friends. "This lady's cousin is over there. We're all going to yell together so she can hear us." He smiled at me. "What's her name?"

I felt rescued. "Lillibette. She's the woman over there with the shoulder-length light blonde hair and no hat. She's wearing a gold scarf and a black jacket."

"Got her." He spun to his friends. "Lillibette. Her

name is Lillibette and she's right over there under the streetlight. "On three. One. Two. Three! Lillibette!"

Nothing.

"Again. One. Two. Three! Lillibette!"

I noticed some of the crowd had joined in that time. Lillibette looked around once then went back to talking to a group of women near her. It never took her long to find someone to talk to. The college guy dragged his cooler next to me. "Here. Stand on this. Okay everyone, one. Two. Three! Lillibette!"

This time, lots of people yelled. Lillibette stopped and looked around… then went back to talking.

"Here." A large, older man with a fleur de lis painted on his cheek handed me a giant Brees foam finger.

"Thanks!" I'd never actually worn one before. I jammed it over my hand and nodded to the college guy.

He smiled. "This time we're going to do it three times in a row. Ready? Lillibette three times in a row. Ready? One. Two. Three!"

I waved the foam finger as dozens of people yelled, "Lillibette! Lillibette! Lillibette!"

Lillibette's smile was huge as she spotted me in the crowd. She waved for me to come over and I shook my head and made an "X" with my arms then pointed to the police with the foam finger. She pointed at herself then made walking motions with her fingers and pointed to me. I shook my head no and pointed at the police again. Then I shrugged. She shrugged back. I handed the foam Brees finger back to the older man then took the college guy's hand as he helped me down from the cooler. "Thank you so much."

"That sucks. She's just right there. Are you alone now? You can stay with us if you want. There's beer in that cooler if you want one."

So I got to know the group of cousins and friends-since-childhood from Chalmette. They swapped stories of the Aints' years - their parents wearing paper bags, getting free tickets to the Dome at the grocery checkout and enduring the pain of loving their losing team year after year. The guy who helped me told stories of grandparents who'd had season tickets for decades and how his Maw Maw and Paw Paw had passed theirs down to him on his eighteenth birthday - just in time for the Saints first NFC Championship season in 2006.

The parade took far longer than any of the organizers could have predicted. Things were at least an hour behind schedule. With the sun set, the air was brutally cold and the near-constant wind was just cruelty. But the crowds were the thickest I'd ever seen and I was managing to stay warm enough to still be glad I was there.

Then, a boy with his boys and another guy with his guys started to argue. With all the blustery talk and chest-puffing, it was clear they'd all had way too much alcohol. The yelling and puffing escalated until the boy finally pushed the guy and the guy started shoving and grabbing. Normally, I would've been terrified to have a giant brawl break out next to me but it felt so wrong for them to mess up our perfect moment. So when everyone sprung to action, I joined in. The guys in the crowd all worked in concert to keep the fighters separated while all of the women stood between them yelling, "NO FIGHTING!"

I was fearless, my face less than a foot from one of the fighters. "NO FIGHTING! NO FIGHTING! NO FIGHTING!" Two police officers rode their massive horse to the edge of our crowd but kept going when they saw we had it all in hand. Everything calmed down and we all went back to laughing and waiting. Then the boy started fighting his own friend. Before we could even react, one of the mounted police burst through the crush of people, grabbed the boy by his hood and dragged him backward through the crowd. The other policeman snatched the friend and yanked him out. The Chalmette group and everyone around us sang *Na Na Hey Hey* and goodbyes as the horses dragged the troublemakers away.

Screams and cheers broke out up the street and we all turned to find the parade approaching. A military band led the way followed by Clydesdales and a very old fire truck. Bands from local high schools and middle schools played different versions of the Ying Yang Twins' Crunk song. One band even did a xylophone version. Adorably-uniformed girls danced and twirled batons or shook pom pons. Everyone from the patient and appreciative elderly to the drunken college kids kept saying how wonderful it was that they included children and students in the parade. "They will never forget this moment."

The first float was donated by the Krewe of Endymion, one of the bigger, well-financed Super Krewes. A giant Lombardi Trophy adorned the front and the Benson family, the Saints' owners, waved at the grateful Who Dat Nation. The Bacchus float carried Super Bowl MVP, quarterback Drew Brees, who looked to be having the time of his life. He led the crowd in chants of Who Dats to the Crunk song. He threw a strand of beads our way and the guy who'd helped me reached up and snatched them out of the air. He balled them up and slipped them into a pocket inside his coat then patted his heart where they rested. "That came from Drew Brees himself. I'm giving it to my Paw Paw."

The floats and bands moved past at a sleepy snail's pace - and they all played the Crunk song. The Saints waved as we took photos of them. We waved as they took photos of us. We were ALL amazed to be there and wanted to remember it forever. The players were drinking and pumped but clearly humbled. I'm not sure if we loved them more or they loved us more. It was an ocean of love and I was bobbing along in it, happy-crying myself silly. It felt like I might fly apart, unable to contain that much joy at once. We all knew it was a once-in-a-lifetime moment.

A Saint waved from the top of a giant Vegas-lighted stiletto that read, "Muses" down the side. I was getting excited to see all these upcoming Mardi Gras parades after seeing some of their floats. One band broke from the pack and played a funky version of *When the Saints Go Marching In* as we sang along. The 610 Stompers, the all male dance troupe from the Buddy D. parade, did their Crunk dance and the crowd went bananas for them again. Then the group I was with started yelling, "It's the Pussyfooters!" as a group of women in pink wigs, black-and-gold corsets and sequined costumes did a fun, sexy dance routine.

A brass band played, of course, the Crunk song. I thought I spotted the tour guide in the gold wig she'd been wearing the other day but it was hard to tell under all the showgirl makeup.

The parade ended with a giant, fanciful train engine. The coach, Sean Payton, lifted the actual Lombardi trophy high into the air and we all squealed ecstatically. It was as if he were lifting the whole city. He looked so happy and grateful and victorious, like a king returning with battle-won treasure.

After the parade passed, the crowd pushed the barricades aside. Our group exchanged hugs and yelled goodbyes and Who Dats as Lillibette and I found each other in the street. We followed the police car trailing the parade. It felt a little like we were "in" the parade for a few blocks until we split off to retrieve Lillibette's car from far beyond the Superdome. She led the way under the overpass. "That was amazing."

I laughed. "Right!?!"

She patted my arm. "Even if we weren't together, I'm really glad you were here for this. I could never have explained it to you."

"I know. I have to try to write about it. It was like the entire Who Dat Nation showed up to say thank you. I met people from all over the place. And the players seemed just as full of gratitude as we were. My entire brain is blown. I'm practically vibrating with joy. I feel drunk."

Lillibette laughed. "Good thing I'm drivin'."

After she dropped me home, I plugged in the tree and turned on the DVR Lillibette had gotten out of her mom's attic. Apparently, *American Idol* had been pushed back an hour locally for live coverage of the victory parade. That seemed a bit extreme for prime time. I went to erase it but got sucked in reliving that once-in-a-lifetime moment for a second time.

Sean Payton held the trophy up for over three hours. At City Hall, *We Are the Champions* played as Payton held the trophy high and the whole crowd sang together. A fairly drunk Mayor Nagin led a toast then a round of "Who dat? WE dat!" Then Payton held his glass high. "Here's to the best Mardi Gras week in the history of this city."

I was so glad I'd decided to stay.

The news said 800,000 to a million people attended. The population of the entire New Orleans area, including all outlying areas, was only 1.1 million. Only eleven people welcomed the Colts home at their airport. The second best team in football, mighty warriors who played hard and finished strong, and only eleven people showed up to thank them. Given that hundreds to thousands of people greeted our Saints at the airport win or lose, week after week, I knew to my soul that at least half of those people at the parade tonight would have stood in that cold for hours, with nowhere to pee or sit, even if the Saints had lost the Super Bowl.

The news said there had been very little crime all week and nearly none that day. Maybe everyone was just too busy having fun to commit crime. Or maybe joy, pride and hope are effective crime fighters. All I knew was that I felt connected to everyone who was there - like we'd all gone to Woodstock or some other otherwise-unknowable experience that bonds strangers forever.

I could actually feel everyone loving everyone. We were all connected. We were all one. After a lifetime of feeling like a stranger in strange lands, I felt like I was part of something. The Saints had somehow reconnected us to our shared indomitable source, our soul. In this city, soul dripped like Spanish Moss from the music, food, people, funerals and celebrations. Now, I felt drenched in soul. Baptized. Reborn.

Chapter 24

The rain finally did arrive and pushed the parade schedule even further out of whack. I was very excited to meet with Mr. Willy but I hoped to be back home before the festivities started shutting everything down. Mr. Willy had grown up surrounded by women in Madame Francine's nightclub and Rick Delaup said he sounded excited to hear a pretty "young" lady wanted to come visit with him.

I knocked on the door of his French Quarter shotgun house and waited. A guy in a standard band uniform (black and white cap, white shirt, black suit and tie) walked past rolling a giant bass case behind him. The door creaked opened and a small white-haired man in his seventies smiled up at me. "Charlotte? Miss Reade?"

"Yes." I extended my hand. "Pleased to meet you."

He opened the door wide. "Come in, come in. Too cold to stand out there for long."

I took my hat off and ran my fingers through my strawberry blonde waves. "Thanks for seeing me."

"Rick told me you were trying to get somethin' this big done during Carnival, I figured you for one of them East Coasters or somethin' but Rick says you've got roots here."

"Yes sir."

He motioned to an elaborately carved wooden Victorian chair with purple velvet cushioning. "Sit, sit. Can I get you somethin'? Coffee? A cool drink? A cocktail?"

"Water's fine."

He disappeared through a series of doors and I took his place in. The furniture seemed mostly passed down from his mother based on the age and level of femininity. There were at least half a dozen photos of a brunette bombshell in fancy, beaded evening gowns. As Mr. Willy reentered, I motioned toward one of the photos. "Who's this woman?"

His face got soft. "My mother."

"She's a knock-out."

He set the water down on a coaster. "Yes she was. Rick says you want to know about The Mermaid Girl. I wracked my brain to remember her name, I really did. But she coulda been goin' by a fake anyway. A lot of 'em did. They'd try to sound exotic or at least sexier than say a Bertha or an Ethel. It could've been Betty. A lot of 'em went by Betty back then."

I tried to mask my disappointment. "So you don't know her name or maybe how to find her?"

He adjusted various pillows behind him on the lavender velvet couch. "She wadn't from here. She was from Biloxi, I think. Somewhere in Mississippi. I remember because there was more than one Mermaid Girl back then and she was the Mississippi Mermaid."

"What was she like?"

He slapped the arm of the couch and a small puff of dust rose around his hand. "Surly. She could be real surly, that one. And she had a sailor's mouth.

Mama hated for the girls to curse. Thought it made us look low class. I think she had personal problems, the Mermaid Girl. She was one of those people who always seemed like they were walkin' in the rain. Like she carried a heavy load."

I laughed. "This is a terrible story."

Mr. Willy laughed too. "You asked what she was like. Shoulda asked what I remember about her 'cause when she got that corset cinched up and the the lights hit her on that stage, she was magical. I'd help wiggle the sheaths of fabric she used for waves. I don't think she ever took any classes but she had a natural gift for dancin'. Her legs were a mile long and when she'd rip the front of the fishtail open and stretch one leg out to the side, you'd think she just dropped money on the crowd."

"So she was well-regarded as a dancer?"

"She was a headliner when she would come to town but she lived on the road. She tried Hollywood but there wasn't much for her out there. I heard she danced in a show in New York for awhile but that might've been one of those stories the girls tell each other like when your parents tell you the family cat is now living on a 'farm.'" He made the quote-marks with his fingers. "Maybe she did. Who knows? She was good enough. She had that thing. Her skin was as velvety and rich as that cushion you're sittin' on and when she did smile, which wadn't often, it lit you up inside, made you feel special or somethin'."

I tried a stab in the dark. "Did you ever hear of her havin' kids?"

"Children?" He looked up to the ceiling. "I don't recall children. Mama didn't like to have a lot of complications. Plenty of women had 'em anyway but it can be bad for business to lose a girl that long, you know? Then they tend to have distractions. Sick kids and the like. Complications."

"Sure."

"I did run into her once with her nieces when she was makin' groceries."

"Her nieces? Two of them?"

"Twins. Said she'd got stuck with 'em when her sister had to go off to work. I didn't realize she had family in town. She'd never mentioned it."

"But they were twins? Identical?"

"A matched set."

"Of complications." It had to be her.

"Little ones. Probably still nursin' age. Too young to be away from their mama for long. I remember thinkin' that at the time."

"Did you wonder if she was lying?"

He laughed. "I never had to wonder if she was lyin'. She lied all the time. Claimed it was a woman's prerogative. Oh, Rick thought you might like to have this." He rocked up from the couch and disappeared through the door again. I heard rustling in the back of the house. I stared at the photos of his mother wishing I could ask her about the sailor-mouthed Mermaid.

Mr. Willy came back in carrying a thick piece of paper. "I lost most of the full size posters and stuff in The Storm but these were in the attic. These were the ones we'd put in the display inside showing who was performing that week." He handed me the paper and I took it carefully on my palms.

I stared down at a black-and-white mischievous

smile, velvet skin and a taffeta and chiffon mermaid costume sitting on a carousel seahorse surrounded by reams of fabric. This was her. I'd actually done it, I found the twins' other mother. I couldn't wait to show them. "There's no way to find her name?"

He gave me a cautioning look. "I don't want to speak ill of the dead," he crossed his forehead and chest with his hand, "And God rest her if she's passed. But that picture is the best of her."

I had to ask. "Has she passed? Do you know?"

Her shook his head. "I'm just assuming. She was a hard woman who needed help softening her edges."

"Drugs?"

"I'd heard there were drugs but I only ever saw the drinking, and trust me, that was plenty to see. She chose her men based on their generosity and tolerance for bad behavior so they tended to be the nouveau riche. All cash, no class. That's what Mama would say. Mama preferred an honest workin' man's dollar any day but she'd take any dollar long as it was green. But the Mermaid Girl? She didn't seem long for this world. Bad choices, hard liven', it takes it's toll. Look, it brings me no joy to tell you these things but that's the truth of her. She was a beautiful exotic flower that only blooms at night in the flood of a spotlight. By day, that flower is cloaked in a tough shell of spiky thorns that can prick and poison if you get too close."

I looked down at the pearls dripping across her arms and intertwined in her hair. Then I looked to Mr. Willy. "How do you think she'd want to be remembered?"

He slapped the arm of the couch again and

another tiny cloud of dust exploded through his fingers. "That's the real question, isn't it? Mama used to say, 'She came, she shined, she drank.'" He laughed to himself. "She did shine. No one can argue that. And like I said before, she was a damn good dancer, real pro stuff. Glamorous without being snooty. And she had a sense of humor in her act too, cute stuff she'd come up with. That seahorse was her idea."

I looked at her sitting sidesaddle on the whimsical carousel seahorse with a twisted brass pole through it.

He gestured toward the photo. "She incorporated it into the act. She would stand on the saddle and use the pole for leverage for these beautiful poses. They didn't used to go all topsy-turvy on the pole like they do nowadays, spreadin' their cha-chas out like shucked oysters. But that was later in the act, after she'd already removed her fishtail. Before that, she had all these moves she's do like bendin' over backward over the saddle and movin' like she was floatin' in water.

Toward the end of the act, when she'd taken off her corset and was just down to the essentials, she did this move in the waves of fabric that looked like she was swimmin' like a dolphin. Then, about the eighties or so, down by where the A&P was - I forget what it is now, the A&P. I don't know what things are anymore, I just know what things used to be. Anyway, whatever it is now, it used to be the A&P."

I offered, "Rouses."

"Yes, well there were these boys dancin' in front of the store and they started doin' her move."

I laughed. "The Worm?"

He laughed. "Is that what they call it? Well, they were on the street with a can for cash doin' that move and I thought of her right away, how that was her move before they were even born. Maybe that was her curse, she was a woman ahead of her time. She was certainly ahead of Jim Crow."

I looked at the photo again, at the seahorse she'd come up with and figured out how to acquire, at the functional and fabulous costume she'd designed and sewn, at her delicately coifed hair with piles and pearls, at her perfectly pointed toes and her elegantly extended fingers. "Maybe so." I stood and extended my hand. "Thank you so much. You can't know what you've done but know that you have my gratitude."

He enclosed my hand in both of his. "I'm glad it helped. I feel a little less crazy about fightin' to save all that stuff all these years through hell and high water."

"I'm so glad you did. It was truly a pleasure and thank you for your hospitality."

I stared at the photo the whole bus ride home. The streets were beginning to fill with parade goers so when I got home, I grabbed my camera and ran to St. Charles to watch Muses, an all-female krewe's parade. It was spectacular. There were big neon butterflies that fluttered down the street high atop poles while other paraders lofted poles with giant neon shoes "walking" high above the street. The giant Vegas-lit stiletto I'd seen at the Victory Parade rolled by carrying the queen. There was a huge bathtub spilling over with giant bubbles. There were bands and dancers and so many throws that a neighbor had to give me a spare plastic bag to carry it all.

Someone yelled, "It's the Pussyfooters!" and I spotted an army of pink-wigged women dancing our way dressed in pink-and-orange burlesque costumes with corsets, fishnets and white combat boots. They were the same group I'd seen in the Victory Parade. They smiled wide as they passed and I realized many of them were closer to my age. Some were older. It struck me as somehow very empowering. They were so strong, feminine, flirty and fun. The old Storyville brothels and the nightclubs on Bourbon might have been long gone but these women reminded me of those women in the Storyville photos, of the Mermaid on the seahorse. They weren't selling sex for money. They weren't even selling their dancing. They were just keeping something alive - a history, an aesthetic, a celebration of the feminine form and the fascinating women who wield it so beautifully.

Back at the house, I set up my camera to download, dumped beads under the tree and plugged it in. I pulled a few toys from the jumble and found branches for them. Then I sat at the card table and stared at the Mermaid Girl photo. I dialed my phone. "Taffy?"

She sounded tired. "Charlotte? What's up?"

"Did I wake you? I just realized how late it is. They had parades all night because of the weather."

She shook the sleep out of her voice. "No, I'm good. How were the parades?"

"It's been amazing. You should come in." I waited and hoped.

"Some people think I already took more than my

fair share of days this year. I can't just be runnin' off now, no matter how good a party y'all havin'.'"

"What about Chiffon? Can she come down from Baton Rouge?"

I heard her pour herself some water. She took a swig. "She's got the kids and she won't bring them down there in all that mess. Says it's too dangerous. It's hard to argue when she's got to tend to them kids by herself and the city is what it is. Why you so hot to get one of us down there? Lillibette ditch you?"

I laughed. "No. I mean, yes, I was alone tonight but you know how it is here. You go alone and make friends on the route. No, I just was hoping you'd be here before I leave next week. I wanted to see you in person."

"You found something."

I smiled. "I did."

She squealed. "I knew it! Didn't I tell you? Didn't I say you'd find her? So who is she? Where is she? Can we meet her? Did you meet her?"

I took a breath. "Slow down. Slow down. I don't know her name or how to find her. I have a photo."

"A photo? But you don't know who she is?"

"Oh, I do. I do know who she is. She's the Mermaid Girl. She was a dancer and that was her act, 'The Mermaid Girl.' I have the photo and I met a man who knew her. I'd love for you to be here before I go so I can make sure you get the photo. I don't like the idea of droppin' it in the mail. It's Friday. Drive tomorrow and go back Sunday night. That way, you don't miss work. We'll go to parades. It'll be fun."

Taffy was quiet a moment. "Lemme sleep on it."

"Okay." I started to hang up.

"Hey Charlotte?"

I put the phone back to my ear. "Yeah?"

"Thanks. Really, thank you."

I sighed. "I just wish I'd gotten more for you."

She sounded misty. "Can you see her face in the picture? Can you tell what she looks like?"

I looked at the Mermaid Girl's hooded eyes, her gleaming grin, her apple cheeks and dainty chin. "Yeah, you can see her. You can tell just what she looked like. She's beautiful. Like y'all."

"Thanks. We never... just thanks."

Chapter 25

I decided to plug in the tree when I woke up and get into the Mardi Gras spirit early. I checked my phone and found a text from Taffy. "On my way. Be there 2ish?"

The parades started Saturday at eleven with the oldest female krewe, Iris. All the riders wore big white masks and gloves in the tradition of remaining anonymous while gift-giving. Between parades, I wandered past families barbecuing on the neutral ground, kids playing jumprope with beads strung together and groups of people doing line dances to their stereos. I was wading through a thick pool of family and community. We had nothing like this in L.A.

I walked back to my spot as the bawdy Krewe of Tucks parade, with its toilet paper rolls and potty jokes, rolled. By the end, the oaks of St. Charles were strewn with toilet paper streamers. The capper was a giant toilet float. My phone vibrated and I checked Taffy's text. "Here."

I walked back to the house and found Taffy sitting in her car out front. I grabbed her bag out of the back and she followed me upstairs. "How was the drive?"

"Sucked. How were the parades?"

"Awesome. There's still Endymion."

She chuckled. "Have you been to that one before?

Their motto is, 'Throw 'til it hurts.' Yeah, they may get a sore shoulder but you gotta protect the head with them boys. Trust me on that, ya' heard me?"

I opened the door and she followed me into the bedroom. She stood looking at the chandelier. "It really does belong here. You know that, right? This is where it used to hang. That's what Mama Heck said."

I startled. "Wait, I thought it always hung in the Treme house. Sassy's house. Mama Heck's house."

"Yeah, after Mama Heck got her house. But when they all first got here, Mama Heck stayed here. It took her a few years to be house-ready. She said the chandelier always had to stay in the family. She said we had to protect it."

"Because it's your family legacy."

"Yeah. But Mama Heck was obsessed-serious about that. Said it always had to hang, never take it down if you don't have to. Don't let it just sit. Don't just store it somewhere and think it's gonna be okay. Keep it hung. In the family home. Mama Heck drilled that into us since birth. Her and Mama both. Honestly, it just makes me feel good seein' it hang here. Like I done right by it, by Mama."

"Paris thinks we're cheating, callin' me family and this your family home. What're you gonna do when I leave?"

Taffy laughed. "You still think you leavin'? You're funny. I still can't believe I left."

I spoke steadily so she'd believe me. "I'm supposed to leave Wednesday."

"Yeah, well, you ain't gone yet. Ash Wednesday? Who schedules anything for Ash Wednesday? Don't leave. For real. Stay. You know you want to."

I chuckled. "I'm trying to remember that you can't pay rent with Mardi Gras beads."

She laughed. "You'll figure it out. You always flower where you're planted."

I had to wonder if that was a common phrase or sign of some sort.

She took my hand. "I have to know. I'm afraid to know, but I have to know." She gripped my fingers. "But don't show me the picture yet. I'm not ready for that, okay?"

"Yeah, sure. Of course. Do you want to go sit down?"

She smiled at the tree as we passed it. Then we plopped onto the couch.

"Where should I start?"

She looked up at the ceiling. "Um first? Okay." She lowered her face to mine. "Where did you get this information? Is it reliable?"

"It's the son of the woman who owned the nightclub where your other mother used to dance sometimes. I'm sure Mr. Willy would be happy to meet you if you want me to try to get Rick to arrange it."

"Who's Rick? Never mind. I don't care. That's good enough. Okay, I guess I want to know who she was."

I took a deep breath. "She was from Mississippi. She was a dancer and she lived a road life. I'm guessing that's why children were difficult for her."

She had her eyes on the ceiling again. "Yeah, I wouldn't have liked to grow up on the road. And then how do you go to school, right?"

"Right. You'd never have even gone to college

much less be teaching it."

She looked at me. "True dat. That's real. What was she like? Was she good at anything? Was she married? Did she have other kids?"

I laughed. "Okay, okay. Um, she wasn't married that Mr. Willy knew of and he didn't know her outside of the club so he wouldn't have known about kids. But he ran into her once when she had the twins with her, you guys. She said they were her sister's but she was prone to lyin' and he'd never heard of her havin' family in town until that moment."

"She lied about us?"

"To keep her job, but she was really good at dancing. Like, really good. Professional. She was a headliner. During Jim Crow. He even heard she ended up dancin' in a show in New York. Maybe it was even Broadway. Who knows?"

Taffy looked like an eager kid. "Really?"

I smiled. "She was a really good dancer. She was beautiful. He said she had a natural gift."

She looked at her hands. "Then I'm glad she got to do her thing, you know? If she was that good."

"He said she was good enough for that. Seriously. He said that she was a beautiful exotic flower that blooms at night in the flood of a spotlight."

She looked up at me and a tear rolled down her cheek. "For real?"

"You should know me well enough to know I don't say things I don't mean."

She laughed and wiped her chin with her sleeve. "I'm good. I'm good for now, okay? Let's just go to the parade."

"Yes!" I jumped up and grabbed my coat from the

chair.

Endymion was a huge Super Krewe. The air was freezing and the wind whipped down Canal Street but the crowds were thick so that helped cut the cold. Saints owner, Tom Benson, was Grand Marshal. The Lombardi trophy sat front and center with him.

The floats were dazzling with tons of lighting effects, like Vegas rolling down Canal Street. Though our frozen fingers stung every time we caught throws, we got so many beads that they were stacked to our ears. My shoulders started to ache on the two-or-so mile walk home. We stopped for a burger and realized upon sitting that there was no way to take our coats off. We were prisoners of our beads.

Taffy played with a glow stick. "You're seriously gonna leave?"

I sighed. "I have to. Don't I? My whole life is there. I know how to make money there. Almost no one in my field figures out how to do that. My world is there. My people are there."

She smacked the table with the glow stick. "Your people are here. L.A. is a place you date. New Orleans is who you marry. You know this. You feel it. I know you do. Look, this place is a mess. Ain't no way 'round that. It's not for the feint of heart and it will break your heart to love it. But I know you feel it. It's got you. You gonna be a never-left."

"A never-left?"

"Ask around how the people weren't born here got here. They don't plan on it. They came for a wedding or spring break or to volunteer after The Storm or whatever and just... never left. All them tourists on Bourbon, they don't know. They never see the city. They come, they drink, they puke, they go. But you been knowin' this place since you were a kid and I seen it back then."

That was the second time I'd heard about never-lefts. I leaned my head back and rested it on the stack of treasures. I thought about what she said, then popped my head back up. "I have an amazing and enviable life in L.A. where I get to do things like go to a party on a yacht in Cannes. My dating pool is *People Magazine*'s fifty most beautiful people. And I really love what I do for money which is such a privilege. And the reason I have all of that is not because I had big dreams, it's because I was disciplined enough to earn it. No relatives in the industry, no blow jobs in bathrooms - I straight-up worked my ass off for it. I gave up things. Big things. I missed wedding and funerals and---"

"But you didn't miss Mama's. She called you home and you came."

I took a breath. "So much of what I do for a living is about waiting, not working. It's about trying to get work. Then lots more waiting. I try to fill as much of that time as possible with irons in the fire, screenplays, producing, even crocheting with Sofia, just to never feel like I'm wasting time. The waiting is pretty-much the hardest part. And there's so much of it. And the way I stay ahead of it so it won't get to me is that I stay industrious. I try not to waste time. I've been here for a couple months and I have to get serious at some point, be disciplined, give up things. The party's gotta end sometime."

She laughed big. "Not here, it don't. Ha! That's funny. Listen. Charlotte, there's a big difference between wastin' time and spendin' time. You been spendin' your time here - and wisely in my estimation. You got an agent and worked on a movie and went to a bunch of parades and, oh shit - you were here for the Super Bowl and the Victory Parade!"

I inserted, "And the Buddy D. parade."

She laughed. "And the Buddy D. parade. And Charlotte, seriously, you found our other mother. You have to know that was time well spent. You did somethin' big for us." She motioned for us to go and we both pushed ourselves up like pregnant women under the weight of all those beads. I laughed to myself as I saw that many of the other diners were prisoners of their beads as well, sweating in coats they couldn't remove.

I wasn't expecting Taffy's hug. Our beads kept us apart like sumo wrestlers struggling to embrace, but I stifled a giggle. Taffy whispered. "Seriously. You were right to be here. If you leave or not, you were meant to be here for this time. Rest in that."

We were bedraggled by the time we got to the top of the tall staircase and inserted the key. I couldn't wait to dump this yoke of beads under the tree. The pile had just hit the ground when Taffy screamed. I ran to her. She was staring at the chandelier with her mouth wide open. I looked around the corner and gasped as well. All of the dangling crystals were pointing straight out horizontally.

Then they began vibrating. Taffy grabbed my arm without ever changing her expression. Then all the crystals dropped and tinkled against each other. All except one. That same one that always teased me.

Taffy stared hypnotically at the one crystal. She let go of my arm and began moving slowly toward the chandelier. She reached her hand out, Mardi Gras beads rearranging themselves around her shoulders. Her fingers extended toward the crystal. The crystal dropped and clinked against the ones next to it. Taffy jumped, jerking her hand away. Then she reached for the crystal again. She wrapped her fingers around it and turned it in the light. "Mama Heck."

"What?"

She looked at me like she'd just then realized I was there. "Mama Heck said they rode this thing from Texas to here in a wagon with wooden wheels and didn't get one scratch on it. Then when they were hangin' it, Mama Heck nicked it with that diamond ring she wore. She showed it to me once. The scratch. Said she never told Mr. Wells or Miss Ruby since they said the chandelier was hers and promised it was. I remember it because the scratch was a funny shape."

Taffy pointed to the crystal and I looked for the blemish. It was easy to find in the light, a checkmark-shaped scratch. Taffy let out a little laugh. "She showed it to me and made a checkmark with her finger, 'Done. You know somethin's truly yours when you can leave your mark on it.'"

"That's a great story." We shared a warm smile. "Are you going to be okay to sleep in here?"

"Now I know it's Mama Heck. She's the only one woulda known which one it was, the scratched one. She's the protector. That's what Mama always said. I'm good with that."

So was I.

Chapter 26

Chiffon called early Sunday morning. My shoulders were sore as I grabbed for the phone. She was to the point, "I'm downstairs."

"You are?" I jumped up and the air mattress knocked Taffy awake. "Get up Taffy, your sister's here."

Chiffon passed right by the chandelier without looking, chattering about the neighbor taking the kids until after lunch. I pulled the foldout chair up into the living room as the twins sat bookending the couch. Taffy grabbed her sister's hands and looked at me. "Tell her about how she was a dancer. A beautiful one. Mr. Willy told her, he's the fella what grew up in the nightclub where she used to dance."

I felt on the spot. "She was a mermaid. She had sheaths of blue and green fabric wigglin' on the floor and she'd come out on a seahorse. It was a merry-go-round seahorse. You'll see it all in the photo. But she made her own costumes and designed her own act. She was multi-talented. She had velvety skin and a smile that lit people up inside." The twins stared at me, their hands clenched. "Mr. Willy said when she danced, she shined. She was magical. And glamorous without being snooty. He said she was a woman ahead of her time."

Chiffon's face was stone. "He really said all that

about a woman that didn't even have enough in her to raise her own kids?"

I searched for the right words. "She musta had her reasons. I'm guessing she had trouble raisin' twins alone with a job that took her on the road."

Chiffon was unmoved. "Then she shouldn'a had kids."

Taffy jerked her sister's hands. "Don't say that. We're here."

I jumped in. "Look, we're never gonna know why she did the things she did, made the choices she made. And maybe if we did, you'd think they were wrong. And then what? There's a saying, 'Rejection is God's protection.' You inherited beauty and humor and creativity - and because she let you go, you were raised with love and attention and stability. Honestly, it worked out okay for you. Maybe it was even for the best. You have to at least allow for that possibility."

Chiffon softened. I got up from the chair and went over to a pile of papers on the folding table. "Here."

The twins reached for the photo together. I left them alone to look take the Mermaid Girl in, but from down the hall I could hear, "She made this herself?" "Came up with the whole act." "I see your smile." "Our smile." I smiled.

The weather had pushed an extra parade onto the morning so Chiffon was able to join us for Babylon and part of Okeanos before heading back to Baton Rouge. After the regally-costumed royal court passed, an Okeanos float rolled by and we all raised our hands for beads. I didn't get any. Taffy and

Chiffon were holding theirs out for each other to see. The "pearl" beads were separated by metallic red beads and little silver seahorses.

I exclaimed, "Seahorses!"

The twins embraced. I looked for the next float as they hugged and whispered things to each other. Chiffon came over and held me a long time, our beads crushed between us, the seahorse strand in her hand dangling down my back. Then she whispered, "Thank you." We waved goodbye to her then turned back to the floats and kept waving for more beads.

Taffy stayed through the colorful tinfoil floats of the Krewe of Mid-City parade and the Egyptian-motiffed Thoth parade. I joined the shouting people around me when I saw the pink army dancing their way up St. Charles, "The Pussyfooters are coming! The Pussyfooters are coming!"

Taffy pumped her fist in the air when they passed and yelled, "Get it girl! Werk!" She hit my arm after they passed, "You should do that. You'd be great. I like how they had big girls. They were ownin' them corsets."

"Taffy, I don't really know if you want to hear this but I feel like I should tell you. I feel like this day has been about your other mother. We started with the photo and then there was an entire parade of seahorses. We literally have a bag full of just seahorse beads thrown to us from floats that had seahorse and mermaid things on them. Now you get to see firsthand how much joy it brings to watch women dancin' in underwear and bringin' sexy back. It just feels like the universe is happy you found your answers."

She smiled. "Metaphysics. Okay. I'll take that." She tipped an imaginary hat to the sky. "I'm happy too." She tipped the hat to me. "I am, you know. I do feel like we got our answers. And I see why Mama didn't want to tell us. We might've longed for her, you know? Some glamorous, sparkly mermaid when our Mama was a regular maid."

My eyes grew wide. "Your mama was no kind of maid. She was my mother's other mother. Her real other mother who diapered and bathed her. She's my other Maw Maw. But I do hear what you're saying. I do. And I think it would've been hard for me not to long for the sexy, elegant woman dripping in pearls and azure taffeta and violet chiffon, riding on a seahorse and shining like a star. I know a little about the seduction of the spotlight-types. But I think we all turned out pretty good, all of us Sassy had a hand in raisin'. She was so good at raisin' kids that she did it for a living. Three generations of my family and two of yours. And it lives on through their parenting when your kids have kids of their own. And on and on. It may not be shiny or sexy or elegant but it's beautiful."

She laughed and wiped a tear. "You gotta stop doin' that. Messin' up my makeup every time I see you. Damn."

I laughed too. "You wanna hear somethin' cool? Mr. Willy said the Mermaid Girl used to do this move where she looked like she was swimmin' in the waves of fabric. He said years later he saw kids doin' it in front of the A&P. It was The Worm."

"The worm? 'The Worm' the worm?"

I wiggled in place. "The Worm."

She laughed. "You're telling me my other mother invented The Worm?"

"I'm just telling you she was doing it in the late fifties. Sixties at the latest. She was a woman ahead of her time. That's what Mr. Willy said when he told the story."

"Okay. I'm out. Drop the mic with that shit. She invented The Worm. I can die happy now. I can't wait to tell Chiffon."

I walked her back to her car, dumped my beads under the lighted tree and ate alone between parades. It was the first time I'd felt truly alone since I got here. I'd accomplished my mission. The story was over. I would be returning to L.A., to eating alone and truly feeling alone. This feeling. But there was another parade coming. So, I bundled up and headed back to St. Charles.

It was dark by the time Bacchus rolled. I'd ignored the fact that it was Valentine's Day all day long. But the Bacchus parade was all about love and hearts and wine and they'd fully embraced the hearts this time. Like every parade this year, everything was Who-Datified. The music, the throws, the costumes, the floats - everything was an opportunity to celebrate our recent victory. Every parade has a king but there were a few kings that meant more to the city than others. King of Bacchus was certainly one of the city's highest honors. This year's king was Super Bowl MVP, Drew Brees.

"Don't know which is the bigger deal, bein' MVP of the Super Bowl or the King of Bacchus."

I turned to find green gloves guy beside me. "Tom." I smiled. "I think it's a big deal squared. They affect each other exponentially."

He laughed a little. "Where's your cousin?"

"She went to Florida, to the beach. A bed opened last minute and she and her common-law jumped at it. I had friends with me earlier but they all had long drives."

He nodded. "How's the ghost? Family secret still safe?"

I felt a small shock, then remembered his tour guide friend. "Safe as ever. I don't even know it. That's how secret it is."

"Well, maybe she'll tell you someday." He looked down at his phone. "I'm way past late. I just wanted to stop and say hi, wish you a happy Valentine's Day. You're welcome to join. I'm meetin' a bunch of friends downtown then we're goin' to head to the Bywater after the parade."

I calculated the miles in my head, how far away from home my evening would end. But I also took in his warm smile and hazel eyes. "That sounds like a long night. I'm gonna stay around here, but thanks."

He took my gloved hand in his green ones. "Until our paths cross again." He smiled and walked away. Over his shoulder, he yelled, "We're at Harry's Corner Bar after the parade if you change your mind. Who Dat!"

"Who Dat!"

Someone else in the crowd yelled it back to me.

After the parade, I called Sofia on the walk home. I told her about the twins and the seahorse parade and about running into Tom as Drew Brees rolled past.

"Did you ask him out?"

I knew she was mostly teasing. "You know I'm

not gonna do that. He did invite me to join him but it was to go walk three miles to a bar full of his friends then walk another two miles to some house party."

"Yikes. That's worse than when you get invited to a party in the hills and end up driving around on one-lane roads all night. Yeah, no. Wait for a better offer. Did he get your number?"

"No. For all I know he was meeting his wife there. People do that here, invite you to things with no intention of tryin' to sleep with you."

"Must be heaven for you."

"Yeah. Kinda perked up my Valentine's Day just knowin' there are nice guys out there."

She laughed. "You mean out there. You already dated all the guys out here and swore you'd never go out with another guy in L.A. You made me sit through that whole I'm-going-to-die-alone speech. Remember?"

"Drew Brees was the king and he's also the Super Bowl MVP and I was thinkin' about that, about how important each of those titles are in their own way. You know, I don't think I have a problem with bein' famous. If I did, I wouldn't have so many famous friends. I think I'm just really picky about what I'd want to be famous for, you know?"

Sofia snickered. "I know you're changing the subject."

"No, but Tom was having thoughts like this too."

"About being famous?"

"No, about being the king and the MVP. But that's not the point. The point is that I wouldn't mind bein' famous for curing cancer or proving a math theorem. I just wouldn't want to be famous for dating someone or for wearing something. Drew Brees rolled by and everyone was starin' up at him and wavin' themselves silly, yellin' out his name and Who Dats and he was up there in his crown and wearin' this gold Renaissance Festival suit throwin' beads and footballs and you could just feel how much joy he's brought this city. I wouldn't mind being famous for that."

"I'll alert the NFL."

I laughed. "I remember George Clooney told me one time that it was hard to be famous for being on TV because people see you in their livin' room. They're wearin' pajamas or underwear and they're used to that - to havin' you in their livin' room while they're eatin' cereal in their undies. So when they see you in the world, he said they feel free to put their hands on him and call him George like they know him. He said with movie stars, people have to dress up. They have to adhere to a schedule, get in their car, purchase premium-priced concessions and find dates to watch with. So when they run into Kevin Costner on the street, it's all please and thank-you and callin' him sir."

"That's true."

"Right? So think of how people treat the person who proves a math theorem. They don't dig through the trash lookin' for pregnancy sticks, I'll tellya that."

She laughed big. "I'm not even math-smart enough to come up with a joke for that. Did you guys talk about anything else? Green gloves guy?"

"The ghost."

"Stop!" She laughed even bigger. "You're right. I'm being nosy. I don't want to hear anymore."

I laughed too. Then I got more serious. "Taffy says it's Mama Heck. And Sassy called Mama Heck 'The Protector.' And Tom said the ghost protects a family secret."

Sofia ventured, "The chandelier?"

"I guess. I don't know. I mean, the wires were tied before the chandelier got here. But, Mama Heck did die in this house."

"Dear God."

"Yeah, but if she protects the chandelier, she wasn't doing a very good job before it got here. So maybe the chandelier has nothin' to do with a family secret. I don't know. Mama Heck had all these rules about keepin' it hung. Not sure what that's about but they all take it very seriously. But then there's the weird thing about it havin' the same symbol as my dad's pipe."

"And the flask."

"What if there really is a family secret?"

"Then you should stay and figure it out."

I chuckled. "Add it to the list. Reason number whatever-the-hell Sofia thinks Charlotte should stay in New Orleans. I'm beginnin'a think you're tryin' to get rid of me."

Sofia got serious. "When I moved to L.A. I knew two people. Now one of them should be somewhere else. That doesn't make me happy. But you sound so much better there. That makes me happy."

"I solved the mystery and did my whole closure moment with two days of Mardi Gras to spare. It's probably a sign to start packin'."

"Enough of the signs. You see what you want to see. Maybe it's a sign that you ran into that guy again. On Valentine's Day no less. Maybe it's a sign that you should be figuring out your family secret. Maybe the chandelier is asking you to protect it. Who knows? Who cares? What do you want? Who do you want to be? And where can you be that? That's all that matters." She sighed. "Just focus on that. Focus on you. Not even your job, just you."

"I am my job. Everything I do revolves around that."

"Then that might be the first thing you want to look at." We were both quiet a moment. "Happy Valentine's Day, Charlotte."

"Happy Valentine's Day, Sofia."

Chapter 27

I'd spent most of Lundi Gras going through all the stuff I'd managed to accumulate in these two months. I decided to wait on un-decorating the tree. It was bringing me too much joy. It was full of toys and beads now with a pile of throws so high underneath that they touched the bottom branches. I wished I could keep it all but it would cost a fortune to mail and there was clearly going to be no room in the one rolling bag I'd brought when I thought I was coming for a five-day week.

The parades that Monday evening were spectacular, especially Orpheus - a parade for musicians, actors and other performing artists. I'd tried to go to bed early afterward knowing that the Fat Tuesday parades were starting at 8am.

The air was brutally cold. A rare dip below freezing. And the parade was really late in starting. I'll admit that as I stood out there alone and shaking, I wondered what in the world I was doing. A woman with thin braids spiral-curling out from under her Saints cap leaned into me. "Bitter."

"The cold? I'm dyin'. This better be one damn good parade to be out this early freezin' to death."

She looked surprised. "You never seen Zulu? This is a good one. Old too. Turn of the century times. But I love 'em all. It'll warm up a bit by the time the truck parades roll."

"The truck parades?"

"Elks and Crescent City. They decorate everything themselves. Low budget so most anyone can ride."

"Is it really expensive to ride in a parade?"

She slapped her coat pocket. "Oh honey, it's thousands. The costumes, the throws, the floats, the cops, the barricades, the clean up crews, the bands, the dance squads, e'rybody gets paid. I heard it costs over a million a year for some of them Super Krewe parades."

I looked at the massive crowds lining St. Charles at "the largest free party in the world." I confessed. "I guess I thought the city paid for the cops and clean up. And I never really thought about the bands and everybody getting a check."

"Yeah, they mostly schools and non-profits so it's good for e'ryone. But you not even seein' the whole tip of the iceberg. All them bands and e'rything, they practice for months gettin' they sets right and they costumes ready. It's a act of love, Carnival."

I thought about that. The floats finally arrived and began showering us with beads. I couldn't help but notice how grand it all was now that I knew it all came from the pockets of my neighbors. There was a newer version of the Crunk song with the Who Dat chant as it's chorus. I happy-cried, singing along with the crowd as gorgeous teenagers danced past in sparkly leotard costumes and majorette boots with big tassels. They had to be freezing.

I wandered between parades. There would be an extra delay since a Zulu float broke down. Someone said it was a fire. I walked past daddies grilling meats, children covered in throws and playing with new toys, grandparents laughing and being tended to in foldout chairs. This is how I'd grown up, all generations enjoying the same things together. The closest you'd get to that in most of L.A. was an older man and younger woman with their baby.

Passing tents of people making sandwiches and doing line dances, I thought about Sofia's questions. What do I want? Who do I want to be? And where can I be that? I stopped and closed my eyes for a second. I promised myself that I would find three whole minutes to not think about work and see what happened. When I opened my eyes, everyone was crossing the street to where they'd moved the Rex parade to get around the Zulu breakdown.

It felt odd somehow to stand on the neutral ground rather than the sidewalk but I joined the crowd and watched Rex, one of the oldest and most respected parade krewes. The floats were much smaller but so pretty. I especially loved the Phoenix rising from flowers and flames. I realized how much these parades were like producing a movie. It takes about two hundred people to make a movie. Some take far more. Everyone is amazing at their specialty and they all contribute to the whole. They make amazing things come together for everyone's entertainment. And, like a parade, people never see the faces of most of the folks who make it all happen.

But it wasn't really like a movie. People make a living making movies. This was more like if the people making the movie also paid for it. And made no profit. And people saw the movie for free. And came home with armloads of gifts paid for by the filmmakers. So, it was actually nothing like a movie. There was no backend.

After the parade, we all crossed the street again, resettling into our original locations. I ate chips and moon pies I'd caught and waited for the truck parades to begin. I tried not to get maudlin thinking about how these were the last parades of the season, thinking about going back to L.A.

I looked up at the beads dangling from the live oaks and decided to try thinking about what I wanted. I wanted to be happy. My phone vibrated in my pocket and I pulled it out. Marilyn.

"Hey, listen, I'm at the parades. Can I call you when I get back tomorrow?"

She sounded impatient. "Can you write this down?"

"It's Mardi Gras. I can eat and catch beads. That's about it."

An older man beside me smiled, "Everywhere else, it's just Tuesday, right?"

I nodded.

Marilyn sighed. "Okay. I'll call you back and leave the details. You've got a really good audition coming up Thursday. It's a small part but it's a great project. I'll leave it all in the message. I already emailed you the sides so you can study them when you get back to your place."

"Okay."

She was stern. "You can work on it on the plane."

"Okay, great." I hung up and slipped the phone back in my pocket then ignored it when it vibrated again for Marilyn's details. I looked back up at the beads in the trees. I tried to put the audition out of my head and think about what I wanted, what would make me happy. But my mind was like a rubber band snapping back to hoping the audition was for a good part. Maybe this would be the one that would finally give me a chance to spread my wings and show off a little. My mind was wondering if the part was right for me. Wondering if I would be in my underwear. Then I wondered about the premiere. Would I finally be able to share a victory with a man or would Sofia be my date again?

I almost got hit by a strand of beads before realizing the parade had started. I raised my hands as the float passed. I caught two strands of beads and hung them around my neck. I watched as a husband draped beads over his wife's head. They laughed and kissed and went back to catching. I wanted that. I wanted someone to do fun things with and celebrate my victories with. And I wanted someone to share my sorrows with. And I wanted it to be someone who thought going to parades was more cool than owning a fancy car or new Prada shoes.

And I wanted to create beautiful things that made people feel good - even if there was no profit in it. I wanted the right to grow old gracefully without feeling pressured to get "freshened up." I wanted to be around people who cared about what I cared about, valued what I valued.

But I valued movies. I wanted to make my mark in movies just like everyone in L.A. I'd lived there eighteen years by choice. And I'd made something of my time there.

As the sun settled over the trees and the firetruck

signaled the end of the parades, I gathered my bags of beads and made my way back to the house.

I dumped the sacks under the lit tree and stood back to admire the season's booty. I snapped the TV on and fixed a plate of leftover red beans and rice. I was starving. *L.A. Story* was playing. I hadn't seen it since it came out in '91 but I remembered it being funny. Steve Martin was talking to a signpost. He walked back to the car and said to Marilu Hemingway, "The sign spoke to me. Said I was in trouble." She retorted, "If you're talking to signs, you ARE in trouble."

Yeah. Sofia was probably right. Signs weren't going to help me figure out what I wanted and that was what I should be focusing on. Steve Martin was roller skating through a museum on the TV. It was an awesome scene. Really well shot, too. Steve's voiceover narrated. "I call it performance art, but my friend Ariel calls it wasting time. History will decide."

My phone vibrated in my coat pocket. I jumped up to grab it. Sofia.

"Hey. I'm eating. Can I call you back?"

"Do you need a ride from the airport or have you come to your senses?"

"I'm torturing myself. You knew I would. I kept waitin' for some kind of epiphany, you know? I did that thing you told me not to do of lookin' at all the signs instead of lookin' inside to figure out what I want. I already know I'm going back so it's stupid to keep hemming and hawing. I'm just teasin' myself with some fantasy of runnin' away and joinin' the circus."

"You mean like leaving everything to go into showbiz? I'm going to quote you. You ready? 'This is not the dress rehearsal. This is your one and only life.'"

I'd said that a lot. Down the hall, I heard the chandelier acting up. What did that dang symbol mean?

Sofia grew impatient. "I'm ending this. Do you have a coin? You're going to do that thing your mom always says to do if you're having trouble making a decision."

"No."

"Yes. You're going to flip the coin and see how you feel when it lands. If you're happy, do what the coin says."

I finished, "And if it makes me go, 'Oh,' then do the other thing."

"Do you have a coin?"

I grabbed a doubloon from the pile under the tree. It was from the Krewe of Bacchus. Sometimes when I was acting, I'd slip something in the pocket of my costume. Just touching it would bring back a flood of emotions and memories. As I turned the coin over in my hand to establish the head from the tail, a wave of Who Dat chants washed over me. I saw Drew Brees waving, confetti flying, families and friends dancing and laughing. No one was thinking about their jobs or how this networking event might benefit them. I saw bands marching and girls twirling batons. I saw Tom waving his green glove as he walked away passing a girl in a Marie Antoinette costume carrying a sign that read "Oui Dat."

Sofia's voice cut through my thoughts. "Ready?

Flip it."

The doubloon hit the ground. I didn't bother looking. "You win."

I had no idea what I was doing and I was pretty sure it was crazy but I was going to try one more bold leap in my life, the leap home.

APPENDIX

These people and places mentioned in the book are real and open for business as of this publishing. For more information on anything mentioned in this book, use the search tool in LAtoNOLA (latonola.com), the blog upon which many of the book's recollections are based.

Cafe du Monde
http://www.cafedumonde.com

Dancing Man 504
https://www.facebook.com/Dancing-Man-504-239176338346/

Rick Delaup (Bustout Burlesque)
http://bustoutburlesque.com

Fat Catz

Fleurty Girl
http://www.fleurtygirl.net

Forever New Orleans
https://www.facebook.com/foreverneworleans

The Gumbo Shop
http://www.gumboshop.com

Harry's Corner Bar
https://www.facebook.com/Harrys-Corner-139022506152999/

Doreen Ketchens (clarinet player)
http://www.doreensjazz.com

Lafitte's Blacksmith Shop Bar
http://www.lafittesblacksmithshop.com/Homepage.html

May Baily's Place
http://www.dauphineorleans.com/nightlife

Christine Miller - Two Chicks Walking Tours
http://www.twochickswalkingtours.com

Anders Osborne
http://www.andersosborne.com

The Pussyfooters
http://www.pussyfooters.org

Rouses
https://shop.rouses.com

Royal Sonesta New Orleans Hotel
http://www.sonesta.com/royalneworleans

The New Orleans Saints
http://www.neworleanssaints.com

Storyville
https://storyvilleapparel.com

Sucre
http://www.shopsucre.com

Tanya and Dorise (violinist and guitarist)
http://tanyandorise.com

Tipitina's
http://www.tipitinas.com

Tujague's Restaurant
http://www.tujaguesrestaurant.com

610 Stompers
https://610stompers.com

These people are gone but you can read more about them on my blog,
LAtoNOLA.

Albert Joseph
https://latonola.wordpress.com/2010/08/05/r-i-p-albert-joseph-jackson-the-moses-of-magazine-street/

Claudia Speicher
https://latonola.wordpress.com/2014/01/30/remembering-claudia-speicher/

ABOUT THE AUTHOR

Best known for her role as Leonardo DiCaprio's sister in Quentin Tarantino's *Django Unchained*, Laura Cayouette has acted in 40 films including *Now You See Me*, *Kill Bill* and *Enemy of the State*. Television appearances include *True Detective*, *Friends* and an award winning episode of *The Larry Sanders Show*.

Laura earned a Master's Degree in creative writing and English literature at the University of South Alabama where she was awarded Distinguished Alumni 2014. She currently resides in New Orleans.

Website: lauracayouette.com
Twitter: @KnowSmallParts
Facebook: http://bit.ly/1VxJIvr

CPSIA information can be obtained
at www.ICGtesting.com
Printed in the USA
BVHW042109240420
578404BV00012B/826